AUTHORS NOTE

This book has been my whole life in the making, but before losing my sister in 2022, I didn't think it was something I would ever do. Losing her brought a new perspective to my life. A perspective that I would trade in a second to have her back, but since that's not an option, I'm going to use it to live my life the way she would've wanted and the way I wish I had lived all along.

No regrets. Take the trip, buy the cottage, eat the ice cream, and write the book.

FOR BEC

Because grief sucks and because you told me to.

Remember when.

One Life TO LIVE

Athena Barnim

ISBN:

E-Book: 978-1-963179-46-0

Paperback: 978-1-963179-47-7

Hardback: 978-1-963179-51-4

CONTENT WARNING

This story includes sensitive subjects, including grief and sibling loss. Please be aware before beginning and make the best decision for yourself to read or not to read.

Always take care of your mental health first.

Contents

CHAPTER *One* 7

CHAPTER *Two* 16

CHAPTER *Three* 21

CHAPTER *Four* 26

CHAPTER *Five* 33

CHAPTER *Six* 42

CHAPTER *Seven* 48

CHAPTER *Eight* 51

CHAPTER *Nine* 55

CHAPTER *Ten* 63

CHAPTER *Eleven* 68

CHAPTER *Twelve* 78

CHAPTER *Thirteen* 86

CHAPTER *Fourteen* 93

CHAPTER *Fifteen* 103

CHAPTER *Sixteen* 107

CHAPTER *Seventeen* 111

CHAPTER *Eighteen* 126

CHAPTER *Nineteen* 137

CHAPTER *Twenty* 150

CHAPTER *Twenty-One* 157

CHAPTER *Twenty-Two* 165

CHAPTER *Twenty-Three* 170

CHAPTER *Twenty-Four* 173

CHAPTER *Twenty-Five* 178

CHAPTER *Twenty-Six* 185

CHAPTER *Twenty-Seven* 192

CHAPTER *Twenty-Eight* 198

CHAPTER *Twenty-Nine* 201

CHAPTER *Thirty* 206

ACKNOWLEDGEMENTS 210

ABOUT THE AUTHOR 212

CHAPTER

One

Jenna

"Okay, my car is packed; I'm on my way out the door! I'll see you soon!" I assure my mom, with the phone wedged between my shoulder and my ear. I'm trying, but it's proving to be easier said than done to actually get out the door of my tiny Toronto apartment for the last time. She can't see that I'm juggling my purse, a box of bathroom cleaners, and a grocery bag consisting of the contents of my junk drawer - all while trying not to drop my phone from the crook of my neck.

I don't even hear her last reassurances...or questions; whatever it is she's saying, I just reply with a chirpy, "Okay, bye, Mom. I'll see you in a few hours."

"Okay, Okay. Bye, Jenna dear; drive safe!"

She finally lets me hang up, and I should be rushing out the door to my car and my new life...or old life. New, old life? I don't even know.

Before I head out of this city for good, before I head home, I set everything down and just stand still.

I feel like this should be a sad moment, or bittersweet at best, but I honestly feel almost nothing. I don't love this apartment anymore. Don't get me wrong, I loved it when I moved here six years ago.

It represented so much to me; a new life, a new job, and my independence from my mother, to name a few. But no matter how much I loved it, I never stopped missing Balsam River. That is where I will always belong, where I will always be at home. Now that I finally recognize that, I know I will never find that feeling here. Not in this apartment, not in this city and not even at the job I fought so hard to make my place in. Marketing has never been where my heart was. I thought I would like to create ad campaigns for major companies and grow their clientele, in turn creating more revenue. It was what I thought I would be doing here for a few more years, but it feels so cold and lifeless when I think of what I could be doing back home.

I need Balsam River, I need my mom more than I will ever care to admit, and I need my big brother, too. If Mark can make his way back to our hometown that he fled so many years ago, then I need to listen to my heart and do the same.

But there's so much more to it than just Mom and Mark, it's everything. There's this whole culture there that is just a part of me. I need it all in my life, and I'm done denying myself. I need Paul's Corner Store, Liam's Coffee and Books, and Kathy's Bakery. And according to Mom, Cara just opened a beautiful Italian restaurant, and soon Jenna's Blooms will be on Main Street with all my favourite small-town businesses! I don't need Toronto to make use of my business degree. I don't need a big fancy office, a hundred floors above the street. I don't need this tiny-ass apartment draining my bank account. I have finally saved enough, living this nothing life in this dirty city to make my way back home. I can open up the flower shop that I always dreamed of when I was a little girl. I can get my coffee at Liam's in the mornings and not have to wait in line for twenty minutes. I can find a cute, little, rundown house with good bones. I can have a backyard with a garden. Heck! I could have a backyard and a front yard! Imagine that! It's the little things. The little things are turning into the big things. Life has thrown so many curveballs to so many people that I love. It's time that I be there for them while we all heal, and I want to be there to deal with any more that come our way.

There's so much purpose for me back home, not just working on accounts that mean nothing to me all day long. Mom can always use help around the house, inside and out. I know Mark could use a hand with little Andria, and I would love to get to know my niece a little better and really build an auntie bond with her. We missed so many years of her life while Mark was gone, and now, he's back, and I'm not there. Well, enough is enough. It's time for a change.

Mark left with Andria right after she was born and didn't come back, even for holidays, until last year. His wife, Amy, died during Andria's birth, and his grief took such a hold of him that he couldn't stand to be anywhere near any memories that they had together. The day after the private funeral service they held for her, he packed up the necessities for Andria, got in his car and drove away. He kept in touch by calling and texting enough that we always knew he was okay, and that Andria was growing and healthy. As she got older, there were lots of video calls, but God, I missed so much. Her entire short life has been so separate from mine. It's just not what I always pictured when we found out Amy was expecting. I want to make the dreams I've had into a reality. I want to be there for my family again.

I'm glad he did what he needed to, to get through that time. I don't know that I could have helped him if he'd stayed; he was so broken and unreachable. It's been six years, and I can't imagine the emptiness he must still feel with the love of his life absent from every moment that he cherishes. I am so happy that he's reached a point in his healing that he was able to return to Balsam River, not just to visit but to put down roots and raise Andi on the back roads and riverbanks that we were raised on.

She just started grade one at Balsam Elementary and is growing into an amazing little woman surrounded by more love than any child would know what to do with. As far as I've been told, anyway. This is what pulls me down daily, that I don't know any of this firsthand. I wasn't there and I'm not there now.

But I'm making sure that changes today!

I want to support my brother; I want to have a relationship with my niece, and I want to reconnect with my mom to make up for the years of distance that living so far away in the city has caused. I know she needs more support than she leads on. She hates asking for help, but I know she's not getting any younger, and she's all alone in that big house. My dad's been gone for a long time; he left when I was ten, and Mark was sixteen, on to bigger and better things, I guess. He just woke up and left one day without any explanation. Mom seemed to have some understanding of his 'why', but she never shared that with us. Eventually, life just continued on. I barely think of him anymore since he obviously doesn't have a thought for how we're making out, but I know the loneliness takes a toll on Mom. She's not elderly by any means, but I don't want to waste any more of the time that I have to spend with her. After the shock of losing Amy so suddenly, no one in our small town takes anything or anyone for granted, but I wonder if that's not what I've been doing by being away for so long. I told myself I couldn't be there before now; I needed to set myself up to be able to be successful in my own business back home, but now nothing is stopping me. I'm going to be there for them and make up for the years that I couldn't be.

I give my head a strong nod of confidence. There's no one here to see it, but it's more for me than anyone else anyway. I'm going home because, from now on, home is where I belong.

I give my apartment one last glance and pull the door shut behind me.

The four-hour drive northwest of Toronto to Balsam River is uneventful. It's October, so the view is spectacular the whole way. Autumn in Ontario is more than a breath of fresh air; it's like seeing colour for the first time. The trees are all various shades of reds and oranges, with yellows and pinks peeking out, too. There are trees for as far as the eye can see, giving the illusion that I'm driving into a mountain range, but I'm not. It's just northern Ontario at its finest. This is a view I could never get without leaving the city. All these trees, lakes, rivers and dirt roads are how I know I'm approaching the town limits of Balsam River. If I roll my window down, I will hear the river rushing over rocks and boulders; it flows right through the outside of town and carries on through the rest of the northern part of the province. Its banks are probably my favourite place on Earth.

I spent so many summers on those banks with Mark and the Ryans, fishing, swimming, suntanning, drinking beer, and any other number of things kids and teens can get up to when given enough free time.

I have so many memories there, though most of them of the boys ganging up on us girls. Amy and Sara Ryan and I were inseparable for those summers, and our brothers loved tormenting us any way they could. Liam and Noah were always with Mark, and the three of them were a wicked team. Even though I was two years younger than even Sara, who is the youngest of the Ryan siblings, they almost always let me tag along, and those were some of the best days of my life, probably all of our lives if I had to guess.

Of course, eventually, we all had to grow up. After Mark and Amy got married, everything in our little group changed; Noah and Mark had both already joined the fire department by then. Amy was working as a cashier at the local grocery store, knowing she just wanted to have Mark's babies and stay home to raise them; she didn't go to college or university. Man, I wish their dreams had come true. They deserved to have them all come true.

Right out of high school, Sara took a journalism course at the community college and started writing for our local newspaper as soon as she graduated. She's since become the manager of the whole paper and is living her best life off the family farm, but still in Balsam River. She had always talked about moving to the city and writing for a big newspaper or magazine, but after Amy died, I don't think she felt she could leave her parents or brothers. Leaving the farm was as close as she got to following her original plans, but I think she's happy where she's at.

I was the only one still in high school when they got married, just starting my last year, but I remember feeling like I was being left behind while they all grew up and started their lives. Now I wonder if they feel like, when I left Balsam River, I left them behind. I don't think I realized before right now that none of the Ryans left town after Amy died, I don't know if they'd always intended to stay local, or maybe their grief rooted them there as much as Mark's caused him to flee.

The same year they were married, Liam bought a shop on Main Street that had been vacant for years and turned it into a café and bookstore. Liam's Coffee and Books, so I won't have to wait in line for twenty minutes. I was so jealous that he just went from working on his family's farm to running his own business without so much hesitation. I always dreamed of owning a shop on our main drag, too, but I needed a business degree and experience in the business world before I could throw myself out there like that. My anxiety would kill the dream before it even started if I tried to do it like he did. Liam never gave anything too much thought, though; he was always the one to go after what he wanted, and he wouldn't stop until he got it. I haven't talked to him in years, but I am so proud of him for making his bookshop/coffee shop dream into a reality.

So, it's fair to say that their marriage created a shift, but nothing like when Amy died the next spring while giving birth to baby Andi. That's when everything changed. Our lives were never the same; every hope, every dream, and every plan were ruined that day.

It still hurts to think about, to remember, the pain and trauma of those first days and weeks. Some days, it feels like it was yesterday, not six years ago, and I can taste the tears that we shed for all the lives that were broken by her death.

I wonder how Mark and the guys are doing these days. He left such a gaping hole in all our lives when he left, but Liam seemed to take it the hardest. He saw it more as a betrayal. Mark was always closer with Noah than Liam, only because they were the same age, I think, but Liam shut down when Mark took baby Andria and left town. I think he just couldn't see past his grief. Losing Amy shook that whole family to its core, and Liam could never come to terms with the way Mark handled it. He closed himself off from the rest of us pretty quickly after that, and to be honest, I haven't been back home for a long enough visit to break down that wall he built around himself.

I've talked to Mark enough since he's been back that I know it hasn't been easy trying to reach Liam again. It sounds like he and Noah picked right up where they left off, but he's always a little vague when he talks about Liam. I'll have to see if I can help with that in any way once I'm settled.

I haven't seen anyone since last Christmas, but even before that, the connections we had were just lost. Losing Amy broke something in all of us. I could never compare my grief to theirs, and I wouldn't anyway, but I think that's why I lost my place amongst them. It felt like everyone lost more than me. But did they? Because I still lost Amy.

Mark lost his wife, his life partner, his soul mate and the mother of his baby. Baby Andria lost her mother. Noah, Liam and Sara lost their sister, their best friend. Mr. and Mrs. Ryan lost their baby girl, and it doesn't need to be said that no parent should ever have to bury their child.

But me...I lost my Amy - kind, loving and always smiling, Amy. My neighbour always looked out for me like she was my sister too. Amy, who became my sister-in-law and confidante, always made me laugh until tears ran down our cheeks, always waited when I fell behind, distracted or picking flowers, told me which boys were worth my trouble and which ones would most definitely walk all over my heart, accepted me even when she didn't understand me, helped me apply to the University of Toronto for business, and believed in me without doubt or question. Amy told me to make sure I come back one day to open my flower shop. She was so much to so many, but God, did she feel like everything to me. I knew that my loss was not more than theirs, though, so I didn't know where I fit into everyone else's grief. So, I left, too. Thinking of everyone I love while driving into town, I can't help but remember Amy's celebration of life.

I saw the whole Ryan family standing there, surrounded by pink roses and all of Amy's favourite things, and my heart split a little more. How can this be what is left of her life?

Liam caught my attention more than anyone else. He looked so broken and withdrawn that I wanted to just wrap him up in a big bear hug. Our eyes locked, and my heart broke a little more. God, I wanted to hold him, and I needed him to hold me. When his eyes met mine, my whole body went hot and then cold. I didn't know what he needed from me, but I had nothing that I thought would help him, so I turned away.

He was always the kindest to me of all the boys. Even more so than my own brother most days. He always had a smile on his face and always gave a helping hand to anyone who might be in need, but he seemed to always be there when I needed him, no matter what. I wished I could do that for him then, but the pain ran too deep. His darkness stood out that day because it was such a stark contrast to the light that was usually Liam. The Liam I knew and loved was gone.

I wonder what he would've said if I had grabbed him and held him like I knew he needed that day. He probably would've looked down at me confused, with his crooked smirk and ocean blue eyes, wondering why Mark's little sister was interloping in their family's grief; nothing about his gaze had made me think I should've been anywhere near them.

My heart still breaks to think of his brokenness. I wonder if he's healed. If he will ever truly forgive Mark. Regardless of what I wanted to do, the reality was that I couldn't even bring myself to speak to him that day.

I talked to Sara for a few minutes, but we'd drifted so far apart before that and there was so much tension with Mark already being gone that I couldn't do much more than give general condolences. I wanted to give her more; I wanted to give her my shoulder to cry on and my friendship to lean on, but instead, I said, "I'm sorry for your loss," and left quickly with my mom on my heels.

Maybe now that I'm back, I can repair some of the damage done to our friendship. We've grown up so much, and so much has changed. I wonder if she could use a friend as badly as I could.

CHAPTER

Two

Jenna

How I ended up standing outside of Liam's Coffee and Books, I do not know. If I could go back and turn right instead of left at the stop light, that would have me walking through the door of my childhood home right now. But no, I am stupidly about to walk into Liam's place of business and order myself a coffee.

Maybe he won't be here. Or maybe he won't be out front.

Yes! I'm sure he doesn't spend his days pouring coffee, he owns the place, he's not a barista, and he'll be in his office or at a meeting with a supplier maybe.

Gah, why do I always freak out at the thought of crossing paths with him? Because he's so damn good-looking, that's why! And he literally played the role of knight in shining armour to me for my entire childhood.

Okay here goes. Big girl panties on.

I pull the door open and step inside. The warmth that envelops me, along with the smell of roasting coffee beans and something sweet, vanilla, maybe. And cinnamon? Mmm, yes, definitely cinnamon, is all in stark contrast to the cold, ocean-blue eyes that meet mine from behind the counter.

"What the hell are you doing here?" His rough, gravelly voice shakes me out of my daze of staring at his eyes. Wait, why does he sound so angry? And why does he look even angrier than he sounds?

Despite the unease that the coldness coming off him has me feeling, I smile brightly. "Hey, Liam, long time no see! I didn't expect to see you here."

"You didn't expect to see me at the coffee shop that I own?" He deadpans.

Shit, he is miserable today. Okay turn up the cheer.

"Ha, funny, but no, I just wasn't sure how often you worked out front. I just wanted to come in and grab a coffee before I tackle unpacking over at the house." My voice comes out a little higher than I intended but hopefully cheerful, covering up my nervousness.

Why am I nervous? Somehow, every encounter I've had with him since I left town six years ago has been short and stilted. Now that I'm feeling his wrath from across the counter, I'm realizing they were also apathetic. How did I never notice that he showed no emotion towards me in the past six years?

Well, gone are those days, I guess, as are the days when he looked upon me with fondness, apparently, because I think I just saw his jaw clench so hard he may have chipped a tooth.

Between said clenched teeth, he manages to say, "Unpack? At *what* house?"

I'm starting to lose my smile; his suppressed rage is really unnerving, considering I have no idea where this is coming from and how, in a town this small that talks as much as these people do, he seems to have no idea that I'm moving back.

Nothing left to do but break the news to him myself. "I'm moving back. I have moved back." *Ugh, I'm annoying myself now.* "Today. Right now. I'm back."

He glares harder as I try to relearn how to speak in full sentences.

"I'll be staying with Mom for now, but I'm going to be looking for a little place of my own. I'm not in any rush, though. I want to find the perfect little place to call home."

"Fucking great," he mumbles under his breath, though I hear it clear as day, as he turns and walks down the hallway to the right of the counter and through a door. The door slams shut, and I jump. I don't know if I'm more startled by this entire interaction or by the sound of the door slamming.

"Can I get you a coffee, hun?" A smiling woman with a cute auburn bob is looking at me expectantly, holding up an empty paper to-go cup.

"Um, yes, sorry, can I please get a vanilla dark roast with oat milk?"

"Sure thing! Don't mind the boss; he can be a little testy. Though I will say, that was next-level tension, even for him. You must have some history, yeah?"

"Uh, yeah, sort of. Honestly, I have no better idea than you what that was about. I haven't lived in town for the past six years and literally just arrived back to settle down here. I guess they've changed up the welcoming committee." I laugh lightly because what else can I do?

"Oh gosh! What a jerk Liam is. I can't believe that's how he'd act when you're just returning home after so long living away." She smiles brightly. "I'm Sherri and I have lived here for a couple of years now. I was passing through one day on my way to nowhere and saw Liam had a help wanted sign in the window. He hired me on the spot after I made him the best maple latte he'd ever had, and the rest is history. I love this town and can't imagine living anywhere else."

"Wow, that's such a great story. I'm Jenna Davis, born and raised here but headed to Toronto for university some years back. I stayed in the city after I graduated to get some experience in the business world, with dreams of opening my own business back here one day. The city life has run its course. I've just been waiting for the right time to make my way back here. Balsam River will always be home to me. So, here I am."

She smiles at me warmly. Man, I really like this girl, and I don't even know her. As I sip the coffee that she just handed me, my eyes widen as the smooth dark roast, with hints of vanilla, runs over my tongue and down my throat. "Holy shit, this is a good cup of coffee." Her smile widens, and her warm brown eyes seem to soften even more.

"Thanks. I really love making people happy. Coffee and books are two things that almost always do that for people, so this is the best job I've ever had."

Yup, I'm going to marry her.

"Can I marry you?" Her laugh reverberates off the walls of the shop, so unrestrained and carefree that it makes me laugh along with her.

As her laughter fades, she quirks an eyebrow at me. "Did you say your name is Jenna Davis? Any relation to Mark Davis?"

"Yes! He's my brother! Do you know him?"

Her cheeks flush a light pink as she says a little breathlessly, "Do I know him? He comes in here every day, and that, my friend, is who I'm going to marry, but I promise I'll still make you delicious coffee."

My jaw drops, incredulous at how this woman just says whatever she's thinking. Who just professes marriage to a man she barely knows?

Okay, I just did, to a woman I barely know, but I was kidding! And this coffee is amazing.

Oh my God, wait. What if he isn't a man she barely knows? She could be dating Mark, for all I know. He wouldn't have necessarily told me, but I'm sure Mom would have, so she can't be; she must not be. Unless mom doesn't know either....

"Are you dating my brother?"

And there's that laugh again, I smile at the sound. "Ha! No, I wish!" She smacks her hand over her mouth. "I'm so sorry to have blurted that out; I've likely freaked you right out on your first day back in town, no less. I am so sorry!" She fans her face but goes on. "I am in love with your brother. I am secretly in love with your brother. I didn't know he had a sister; I actually don't know anything about him other than he's a single dad to little Andi, who is the sweetest little cupcake to ever come through those doors." She points to the doors behind me. "I think he has got to be the hottest, kindest, softest-spoken man I've ever met and...I'm in love."

I can't help but burst out laughing now. How can she be talking about Mark? He's definitely not hot, yuck. He isn't a jerk, but he's not super kind to people he doesn't know either; he's a little rough around the edges and abrupt if I had to say one way or the other. Honestly, I would say he's more likely to act the way Liam was just acting. The way Sherri just described my brother is exactly how I would describe Amy and Sara's brother, Liam Ryan: hot, kind and soft-spoken. How much has changed in the years I've been gone? How much did grief ruin these guys and everything else that I know to be true?

After thanking Sherri for the best coffee I've ever tasted and making plans to be back tomorrow to chat some more, I head back outside into the autumn breeze to make my way to my car. I forgot how much colder it always seems here. You wouldn't think 4 hours north could make that big of a difference in the climate, but it definitely does! Maybe it's because there aren't any skyscrapers to block the wind, but the chill just goes right through to my bones. Thankfully, it is surprisingly sunny for this late on an October afternoon, so I'm not complaining. I'll take any warmth I can get after that frigid welcome from Liam. Shaking my head, I slide into the driver's seat of my car and head back to the stoplight to make that left turn to head towards the edge of town.

This is right where I need to be, headed towards my childhood home. My mom's few acres full of farm animals disguised as pets and veggie gardens to feed an army is just what I need to calm my now fraying nerves. I can conveniently put out of my head that my mother's beautiful property is situated right beside Liam's corner of The Ryan Family Farm.

CHAPTER

Three

Jenna

"Oh, sweetie! I'm so happy you're here. How was your drive? You're having coffee this late in the day? Is that a good idea? Oh, you were at Liam's? Did you see him? How is he doing? I never see anyone anymore; I just don't get out enough. I guess I have enough here to keep me busy, but sometimes I wish I got out more. Taryn is always telling me that I need to get out more. Can I help you with your things? What can I do?"

"Mom, chill. I'm good, I got it. The drive was beautiful, as always. I need the coffee to get through this," her face falls, so I quickly wave my hand towards my stuff behind me and add, "The unpacking, I mean. Yes, I stopped at Liam's, yes, I saw him, he's fine... I guess, and yes, you need to get out more. Let's work on that now that I'm home."

I lean in for a quick hug and kiss and head back to my car to grab more boxes. Hauling boxes into the garage and some into my childhood bedroom with my suitcases is a little depressing. What had felt like a fresh start and a step toward my future is suddenly feeling like ten steps backward into my youth. What am I doing here? Can I even do this? Mom is going to drive me crazy! How can we reconnect if I can't get enough room to take a deep breath?

As if right on cue, Mom pokes her head in my bedroom door. "Sweetie? Are you hungry? I'm making a snack. If you want some, I'll make extra."

I exhale, exhaustion leeching out into the room. "Sure, Mom, thanks."

Ready-made food isn't a terrible perk to living with my mom again. I make sure to smile at her warmly so she knows I appreciate her asking. This is going to be even harder than I thought if I have to tiptoe around her feelings every day. She has the biggest heart and is always doting on Mark and me. I can't even fathom what it's been like for her here with us both gone. What was I thinking, leaving her for all these years? Here comes the self-inflicted guilt trip. Ugh, stop.

I stand up to follow her downstairs, pushing thoughts of the past out of my head. I'm here now, and that is what matters. Onward and upward.

In the kitchen, I sit across from Mom at the little table she's placed where the larger one we all sat as kids used to be. She always said the big one was too big for the three of us, so as soon as Mark moved out, she sold it and bought this little two-person café style set. I think the larger table without my dad sitting at the head of it may sting a little, but what do I know?

I sit across from her now and can't help but notice how much older she looks; I don't mean that in a bad way, just in a natural, 'she's aging' kinda way. I think I forgot that as I'm getting older, and so is she.

"Mom, I hope you know that I'm here for good now. I want to help out around here even after I get my own place; you don't have to do everything yourself."

"Oh Jenna, don't be silly! I have Mark to help out, and besides, I like fending for myself. It makes me feel useful."

"I know, I know, but you're getting older, and I don't want you to be overdoing it."

"Getting older?" She presses her hand to her chest in mock outrage, "You mean to tell me that my children are thirty and twenty-four years old, and I'm not still thirty-five? Since when?" She laughs and stands to make the tea she boiled water for.

"Come on, I don't mean to insult you. I just mean that I love you and want you to be able to take it easy."

"I hear you, honey; just having you close by again is a weight off my heart, but you better not be moving back here on my account." She glances back at me sternly.

"No, I'm here for me. Trust me. I'm so excited to find a place to open my flower shop and then find a cute little house to settle down in. My being here for you, Mark and Andi are also for me too, though, Mom, I miss the connection we had. I want to get back to how we were before I left."

"Oh, my darling girl, you're all grown up now and don't need me the same way you did back then, but there's nothing I'd love more than to spend more time with you and learn the ins and outs of your heart and mind that I've been missing these past years. Tell me, what pushed you out of the city? Why did you decide to come back now?"

I smile. This is what I wanted. I want to share my life with my mom again, and not just over the phone, but over tea at the kitchen table.

"Well, it was a combination of things really. The rat race that is working in my office was really getting to me. You know, marketing was never my dream, but I thought that I could enjoy it for a time, but that just never happened. My heart was never in it, and I was working so many hours each day trying to keep up with the next guy, how many accounts and how much money, and none of it made me truly happy. I thought I didn't have time for friendships or boyfriends because I wanted to work more to get more experience and save money to do my own thing, but then I realized I was missing out on life while planning this life that I was never letting happen. I just decided one day I'd had enough planning and saving and being unhappy with myself. It's not that I didn't know what I wanted to do. All this time, I was just too scared to do it."

"That's very brave of you, Jenna; you're not scared anymore?"

I bark out a laugh. "Ha! No, I'm scared shitless, Mama, but I'm not letting that make my decisions anymore. I'm here because this is where I want to be, and I have a plan to grow and develop a business that will add beauty and joy to not only my life but to the whole town."

"I can't wait to see it all come together! Here's your tea, and I'll just slice some of this banana bread to go with it—"

"Hello?" a voice calls from the front door.

I jump up from my chair at the kitchen table so fast it almost flips over backwards. I would know that voice anywhere.

"Mark!" I run to the door where he's toeing off his boots with a beautiful bouquet of carnations and roses, in the most vibrant fall colours, in one hand and a tiny hand that still has little knuckle dimples in his other hand. The sight warms my heart.

"Andi!" I wrap them both up in a big hug, crushing some flower petals, knocking Andi into her dad's side, and almost plowing Mark to the ground. I couldn't care any less, though; these people are my heart, and they're here.

"Gosh, you're getting so tall. And your hair. When did it get so long? Look at how mature you're looking, all grown up with these cute boots." She's wearing the cutest little brown leather ankle boots with the tiniest heel, perfect for any six-year-old to feel like they aren't a baby anymore. "Andi, how long ago was Christmas? You've clearly aged five years in the last ten months."

I've let go of Mark now, and I can't stop staring at my beautiful niece. While I hold her shoulders an arm's length in front of me, she smiles shyly at me. "Hi, Auntie Jenna. I'm in the first grade now! Daddy bought me these new boots for my first day of school, and I wear them every day."

We Facetime every week, but these boots never made it to the screen and that has me thinking how much Facetime would never have been enough. I've missed so much already, and I am so happy to be home that I can't stop the face-splitting grin that I'm wearing.

"What am I? Chopped liver?" Mark looks down at us with his classic.

'Poor me. Everyone loves the cute six-year-old more than me' pout.

I jump up from where I'm crouched on the floor and throw my arms around his neck.

"Oh, hi, big brother! No, never! God, I've missed you! Speaking of, though, why are you guys here? Isn't it a school night?"

Mark leans back to look at my face and says, "Like we could have Auntie Jenna moving back to town 'to stay forever." He imitates Andi's little voice, "And not greet her on her first night! School night, schmool night. We had to come to see you."

I can feel my eyes starting to water, and my heart feels like it's been warmed by the fire. This is why I'm here; this is where I'm loved, and wanted, and needed. This is where I belong.

"Oh no, Jenny, don't cry, it's a happy day, the best day! We're so happy you're home. The prodigal son *and* daughter have returned, and you can take some of the heat off me. This town could use something else to talk about." He pulls me back in for a tight squeeze, and I inhale his scent, clean laundry and the same cologne he's worn since high school, something with bergamot, I think. Smells like love and comfort and home. Smells like my brother.

CHAPTER

Four

Jenna

The morning comes too soon, but I have a long list of things to accomplish today, so I jump out of bed with way more enthusiasm than I actually feel. I have a meeting with the landlord of my future flower shop at ten o'clock and then a meeting at one o'clock with Jamie, he's the only real estate agent in town so if I want to find my own place he is where I need to start. I actually thought that he owned the old drugstore that I'm hoping to rent for my shop, but when I called him, he said he had sold it a few years back. He set up my meeting with the new owner, but I'm pretty sure he didn't mention who it was; if he did, I'd forgotten. That's weird, though. In this town, it's obviously someone that I know. Mom never mentioned any of this behind-the-scenes gossip when I was getting my weekly Balsam River updates. I feel so out of the loop. Oh well, I will find out soon enough. But first. Coffee.

I'm not sure what to expect when I push through the door of Liam's Coffee and Books an hour later, but Sherri's warm smile and bright eyes are all that greet me.

Bless her.

I nervously look around the shop. I can't see behind the bookshelves that crowd the back corner, but the rest of the shop is a pretty open concept. I doubt Liam is hiding behind bookshelves. Ugh! There I go again, worrying about Liam's whereabouts.

Why do I care?

I don't care.

I'm bound to run into him again, with coffee this good, likely quite often. So, we will have to just get over whatever this weird, cold awkwardness that we've got going on is. I exhale a breath I didn't even know I was holding and walk up to the counter to place my order.

Sherri hands me a very large steaming cup of coffee.

"Oh! Gosh, thank you! You remembered what I ordered yesterday?"

"Oh no, I'm not that good; I made you my favourite morning wake-up: flat white, oat milk with some cinnamon dolce. All the pick me up without the cramps." She winks at me.

Oh my God, this girl. I just know we'll be friends. I burst out laughing and sip her decadent morning surprise. Yup. She's good.

"Oh my God, Sherri, you're a magician."

"Nah, I just love coffee, and being the reason someone makes the face you're making right now is the best start to my day."

"Well, mine too. So, thank you again."

"I saw you sussing out the place. Are you looking for the Boss Man?"

My cheeks flush pink. I've been called out, but she doesn't need to know that. "No, I- I was just noticing how much light comes in the front windows. Such a great place for those tables over there, with the bookshelves lining that exterior wall, the aesthetic is just perfect."

"So, you were looking for Liam. He's not here. He left just before you came in and said he'd be back in an hour or so; just had a meeting down the street."

Now, my face is a shade of red that I know is not flattering. Damn, this woman and her intuition. "Honestly, Jenna, you're not hiding it well. You've got it bad, yeah?"

"No! Who...? Me...? I was just... Ugh, fine, he's hot, OK? He's hotter than he was when I left six years ago, and he's hotter than he was ten years ago when I was fourteen and thought I knew everything. And that is saying a lot because he was damn good-looking back then, and I may have been in love with him when I was a teenager. But damn, he was so rude to me yesterday; I know you may not believe this, but we used to be friends. I was just so caught off guard by his attitude that I felt like I didn't even get a chance to admire before he stormed away. I really wanted to reconnect with old friends now that I'm back, but I don't know where to start with Liam. Especially when it seems like I've offended him in some way that I am completely unaware of, and now I'm rambling; I am so sorry. I know he's your boss, and I probably shouldn't be telling you all of this." I cover my mouth with my hand, "Oh God! How well do you really fit into this town? Please tell me you're not in with the town gossips."

Her larger-than-life laugh rings through the coffee shop again. And again, it's a lovely sound; it doesn't make me feel self-conscious or embarrassed. It's wonderfully obvious that she's not laughing at me but more that she understands exactly the mess I've found myself in. And it is a little bit hilarious.

Life was supposed to be simpler moving back here. No lineups for coffee, dirt roads, animals in the yard, long days selling flowers to locals I've known my entire life. How have I already got myself into this tangle of emotions and misunderstandings? With none other than Liam Freakin' Ryan, of course.

How can this be happening to me?

Liam is here, standing in my flower shop. My future flower shop... whatever, same difference.

Why is he here?

I remember Sherri's words, *"He's not here. He left just before you came in and said he'd be back in an hour or so. Just had a meeting down the street."*

"You are my landlord?" My hand claps loudly over my mouth again. Why do I keep needing to insert my foot in my mouth today? It's just that I did not mean to say that out loud, at least not in the tone that it came out with. Shit, I'm really screwing this up.

"Not yet, I'm not." He grumbles

"I'm sorry, Liam. I didn't mean that how it sounded. I just meant I didn't know you owned this building now. Jamie didn't say who he'd sold it to, just that he had a few years---"

"And how did it sound, exactly?"

"What?"

"You said you didn't mean that how it sounded. How did it sound?"

"Oh, I...I don't know, angry I guess... Disbelieving, maybe...but snarkier than I intended. I just feel like we've gotten off on the wrong—"

"Oh yes, high and mighty Jenna, back from the big city and doesn't know all that there is to know. Poor Jenna."

"Okay wow. First of all, interrupt me one more time, and I will call your mother right now. Secondly, what is wrong with you?"

"What is wrong with me, Jenna? You are what's wrong with me." The heat in his eyes doesn't match his indifferent tone. This guy is the walking definition of hot and cold.

"Liam, I honestly have no idea what you could be talking about. What could I have possibly done to you in the last six years? For shit's sake, Liam! I have barely spoken to you in the last six years, so whatever your issue is—"

"She's a slow learner here, folks."

"I know you did not just cut me off again."

He raises his hands. "Okay okay. Don't get my mother involved. She loves you and will definitely take your side. I don't have time for that today. I think we're done here anyway. I can't imagine having interactions like this every time I need to check on my property or collect rent from my tenant." He turns towards the door and holds it open as he stands to the side.

He's escorting me out? What is happening right now? I can't let this end this way, but what else can I do? I'm stunned, staring at the side of Liam's face as he ignores me, he's waiting for me to leave 'his shop' and I don't even notice Sara walking past the front window. That is until she steps into the entryway and stares at me while I stare at her brother. I blink and turn to look at her. The look in her eyes isn't overly friendly either. What is with this family?!

I smile tentatively and take a step towards her. I watch as her brown eyes soften from a little wary to something closer to curiosity and then, finally, warmth. I can almost see our childhood memories flit across her mind. She opens her arms, and I step into her hug.

"Jenna...." She says my name so softly I wouldn't even hear it if I wasn't pressed against her shoulder.

"Sara." I pull back slowly. "Hi."

"Noah said that Mark said that you were moving back. For good? I didn't know when. Wow. It's so good to see you." She shakes her head a little, "I'm sorry, I'm just a little surprised. It's been so long."

"I know, don't be sorry. And yes, definitely for good."

Liam scoffs under his breath from just behind me. I somehow forgot he was here, but now his seething attitude is thrown right in my face again. I glare sideways in his direction. "I'm so happy to be back! I'm planning to open up a flower shop and was hoping to rent this space. It's so perfect, with Liam's Coffee and Books right down the street, Paul always says he can never remember to keep fresh flowers in the store, and with Cara's new restaurant right across from Paul's, I thought it would be a perfect one-stop date night on Main St. We'd be offering the whole package right here, you could have dinner out at Cara's, stop at Kathy's for dessert, grab a coffee from Liam's and flowers before or after to complete the evening."

"Oh, Jenna, that sounds so wonderful! I'm so happy for you! I used to love the flowers you always picked on your way over when we were kids. You always had such an eye for the colours."

Liam clears his throat, not hiding his annoyance with our ongoing conversation. It's as if Sara just realized her brother was standing there, her eyes widening, "Liam! What are you doing just standing there? Are you going to help Jenna get this place set up to suit a flower shop? It's hard to see it the way it is now, but I have faith in you guys."

His complexion noticeably pales, and I can't help but smirk. Is Liam Ryan being put in his place by his little sister without her even trying?

"Uh, well, we.... Uh...we just finished up a meeting, and this space isn't going to work for her."

"Excuse me? I would give anything to rent this space, Liam; you shut me down before I could even show you my business plan." I hold up the folder I've been hanging on to tightly this whole time. "I have a credit check, references and a detailed business plan, including computer-generated images to show you what I have in mind for the aesthetic of the shop."

Sara looks back and forth from me to Liam and then back to me again as a crease appears between her eyebrows. I can tell she's as confused as I am as to what's going on with Liam. Thank God I'm not alone on this life raft. "Liam, what's going on? Why aren't you signing a lease agreement with Jenna right now? This is a great business opportunity for Balsam River, and you've been stressing over this place being empty for over a year."

Now, I'm even more confused. He's stressing over renting this place out and still won't rent it to me. I need to get to the bottom of this. And fast.

Something that can only be described as a growl escapes his throat as he lets go of the door that he's been holding this whole time and stalks out onto the sidewalk. Without looking back, his long strides carry him three doors down to his coffee shop, and he disappears inside without a single glance.

I stare at Sara as she stares at where her brother had just been on the sidewalk. "Please tell me that you know what is going on with him and why he is being this way?"

She sighs as she turns back to look at me. "Honestly, Jenna, Liam isn't the same guy that you knew six years ago. None of us are the same. Not just in the 'it's been six years, and we've grown up' sense. I mean, losing Amy changed us. Nothing has ever been the same and never will be again. One year didn't change that, and neither did six. We are forever altered; maybe you didn't see it on your short visits back to town, but that is the reality. I don't even remember who I was before she died. What did it feel like to not have to walk around with a gaping hole in my heart? What was it like to think of her and smile every single time instead of crying? What was it like to be able to call her or go see her whenever I wanted? To ask for advice when life got tough? To laugh with her when life was nothing but a long chain of things to laugh at? I really don't know. I don't know that girl. Liam is in the same camp; we lost our sister Jenna, a piece of ourselves. He is not who he once was, and you may have to take the time to get to know him all over again."

"God, Sara, I'm so sorry. I know all of this. I do. I've been so insensitive. I know it's different for me. Don't get me wrong, I loved Amy, but she wasn't my sister, and there's nothing that I've ever felt that can even come close to understanding your pain. On top of that, I left all the memories here. I got to handle them in small doses when I was ready to, whenever I came home to visit. I'm so sorry if I've hurt you in any way by my actions."

Sara smiles warmly. "Maybe that's a conversation you need to have with Liam." She takes my hand in hers. "I've missed you, Jenna. It's so good to have you back."

CHAPTER

Five

Jenna

It's been two weeks since I met Liam in his—my flower shop, and unfortunately for me, I can't seem to build an argument against Sara's claim that I need to seek him out and have a good talk with him. I'm going to have to put my pride aside and speak with him about where I've been, literally and emotionally.

Chatting with Sherri is like free therapy. I've been able to get some of the thoughts about Amy and Liam off my chest. "Amy's death showed us all that life is precious and that we don't actually have any control at the end of the day. I think sometimes it takes a tragedy for you to see how fragile life is."

I've come to the coffee shop every day and spent Sherri's breaks sitting in the corner chatting with her. She is the kindest soul, and she makes a mean cup of coffee. She is truly a gem, and I don't know what I'd have done this week without her insight and friendship. I don't usually make friends this easily; I had a lot of acquaintances in Toronto, but no one that I would call a true friend. Sherri is different, she's so warm and open that it's hard not to be the same in return. I don't know if I realized until now how closed off I was all those years in Toronto. How did I not have any close friends in *six years*?

My thoughts wander to Mark and how he left everyone else that he loved after having the love of his life ripped from him. I guess, in a way, I did that, too, but I had always planned to go to the University of Toronto. I just went a few months early....and didn't come back when I was done.

"It's clear to me that Liam isn't the warm, carefree, loving guy that I remember. But maybe that's what grief did to him. Maybe he doesn't let people in anymore for fear of losing them like he lost his sister." Sherri nods her head in understanding, so I carry on with my train of thought. "I think experiencing that loss is why I didn't make any close friends in Toronto. Maybe I did the same thing that Liam did, but I did it where no one could see. But, in my defense! I didn't shut out the people of Balsam River. I just didn't let anyone new in."

"Really? You didn't shut out Balsam River?"

"No, I came home a few times a year and always frequented the shops and caught up on the town news."

"Jenna, coming in for coffee isn't the same as maintaining a friendship, and besides, I've worked here for two years and have never seen you. When was the last time you chatted with Sara? Before this week, I mean?"

Shit, do I ever feel called out again. "Well...I don't know exactly, but it's different with the Ryans; they were grieving, and I didn't want to intrude on that. And then, too much time passed, and I didn't know how to find my place with them again. With Mark gone, it didn't really feel like I had a place there anymore."

"Weren't you grieving too? Aren't you still? When I see you sitting with Sara, sharing a cinnamon bun over coffee, sometimes you both get a lost look in your eyes. It's fleeting, but you're both wishing Amy was sitting with you. I see you both laughing over at bookshelves as you choose your next read. I hear you making fun of the cheesy romance covers, but then your laughter peters out to silence. You both remember doing the same things with Amy when she was alive. That is grief. It doesn't go away, but it's also not always front and centre. It comes out of nowhere and punches you in the gut, a fleeting memory, just a little yearning for her presence, for the way things used to be. It doesn't mean you're unhappy; I know you're not. I see you smile, and I hear your beautiful tinkling laughter and Sara's, too. Grief shows up in the love that you still have; you'll carry it forever. Six years won't make it go away. Fifteen years won't make it go away, and moving to a city four hours away and ignoring everything that hurts too much definitely did not make it go away either."

With tears running down my face, I reach across the table and grasp Sherri's hand. "I don't think I've ever felt as seen as I do right now. Thank you." My voice cracks with emotion. "God, Sherri, thank you for everything."

"Oh, honey, I just want to see you put these two families back together. I've seen Mark and Liam reconnect over this past year, and like I told you, I don't know Mark that well, but I can see the lightness in him when he brings Andi in, and I can see the love pour out of Liam when he comes out to greet them. That little girl could shine the wax off a candle. She's just the brightest light in all of this, and it'd do you all good to take some lessons from her."

"I think you're right; I could take some lessons from Mark *and* Andi. I need to talk to Liam and see what I can do to bridge this gap that's come between us. There's no reason we can't be friends again, we used to be close, you know? I think I was just so happy to be back and starting fresh that I didn't give everyone else around me the chance to adjust. Although Liam seems to be the only one who's struggling with that adjustment, I'm sure a conversation can clear the air, and we can start over, too."

I quickly glance around the shop and behind the counter, looking for him, no sign of him though. "Is Liam here, in his office? I don't want to let this fester any more than it already has."

"No, he's down the street at the vacant building. He said something about a fresh coat of paint to get it rented out faster."

Ugh, that man! I can feel my anger rising just at the mention of him not renting me that space like he doesn't have a willing tenant right here! I take a deep breath. It's okay. I will get to the bottom of his attitude problem, and hopefully, we can come to an agreement about the store. As I get up from the table and grab my purse to go find Liam, Sherri rests her hand on my forearm. "Grief is far-reaching, my girl. Don't minimize yours because it's different from his. Different, but still very real."

I have shared more with Sherri in these few days than I've shared with anyone since Sara, Amy, and I spent our summers on the riverbank. As I walk down Main Street to find Liam, I can't help but get lost in memories of our last summer, all of us together, before everything changed.

We spent every afternoon during the week and all day on weekends swimming and fishing in the river. Sometimes, we'd cliff jump or swing from the rope that had been hung from a tree way before our time but somehow still held strong. Sometimes, we just lazed in the water on floaties. We were always together and always happy. Those carefree days were truly some of the best of my life. I cherished them even before I knew they'd be some of the last summer days spent with Amy.

I remember hiking to the highest point along the banks, and everyone jumped off one after the other. No one gave a second thought that I hadn't jumped from some of the lower points that we often frequented. I always just slipped in off the bank and carried on swimming with everyone just the same. I don't know why I even made this hike with them; I knew it would be too high. My fear of heights was paralyzing, but now that would be made obvious, I needed to decide how much I cared if they were going to laugh and poke fun that I wouldn't jump. I was just about to turn back and hike all the way back down when Liam grabbed my hand, saying, "Hey, where you going? Water's this way."

"Ha! Ya, no. I'm not going to jump." I tried to keep my voice even, which was more difficult than you might think, with Liam Ryan holding my hand. It's not like we'd never touched before. He hugged me almost every time we

said goodbye after hanging out, but with everyone else down in the water, it was just him and I, and it felt altogether too intimate. This high schooler had a crush that had been only growing stronger as the years passed by. Didn't help that Liam only got hotter as the years passed.

At least he's consistent.

His blue eyes were staring at me now, and it was like looking into the depths of the ocean, that weird turquoise ocean water you always see in vacation pamphlets. Were they somehow brighter today?

"Oh, come on, Jenna! You have to jump! I can't go by myself." His mouth tipping just slightly into a smirk was enough to make my stomach summersault. Was I falling through the air right now? No, I'm standing on solid ground. Just falling more in love with Liam Ryan with every word he says to me.

"Sure, Liam, 'cause you haven't jumped from this point a hundred times already?"

"Never with you. Today's a first for that, and I don't want to miss out."

Holy shit, I knew he was a charmer, but I don't know if it's ever been directed at me. Being charmed by Liam Ryan is like being struck by lightning.

Why is he being so nice to me, though? Does he know I'm scared shitless and just trying to save me the embarrassment? I think Liam has made that his life mission. If he's not saving me from failed brakes on my bike, he's rushing to the store to buy hair dye to cover up the awful pink that Sara put in my hair last summer.

"Liam, why do you care?"

He looks at me as if I just asked him to fly to the moon. Confused, maybe a little insulted.

"Why do I care about what?"

"You obviously know that I'm too scared to jump, and you're trying to make me feel better about that. Save me the embarrassment of hiking back down and everyone knowing I'm chicken shit. But why? Let me be scared and embarrassed. It's fine; you don't have to protect me."

"Jenna, I don't care what anyone down there thinks of you, or me for

that matter. But I will always care if you're scared or uncomfortable in any way. If I can do anything, big or small, to make it better for you, I will. I will always protect you."

My jaw might be on the ground; I'm not sure.

He flips his brown hair, naturally lighter from the sun, out of his eyes and drags me forward a few steps. He says, "Now let's go. Are we jumping together or what?"

Before I can give it any more thought, I let him drag me by the hand to the edge, and I look at him and whisper, "Thank you."

He smiles that mega-watt Liam smile, counts to three, and we jump. Hand in hand, I'm afraid to even think about it, but I think he's also holding my heart. I have never felt more alive, flying through the air with Liam tethered to my side. His promise to always protect me was imprinted on my heart.

I snap out of my memory-induced coma and recognize the front window of the storefront I'm standing in front of. The window that I so badly want to call my own. I would be lying if I said rebuilding our friendship was the only reason I hoped I could convince Liam to put the past behind us. I also would love it if turning this storefront into a beautiful flower shop could be a side effect of this conversation.

Looking through the window, I can see Liam reaching over his head, taping the edges of the ceiling, getting ready to paint. Nice to see he still fills out his Wranglers better than any model I've ever seen on a Wrangler ad. I can't help but let my eyes wander to how his t-shirt fits across his shoulders in just the right way so that I can see every muscle rippling as he reaches up and tears off the tape. How can painting a damn wall look this sexy?

Jeez, Jenna, get a grip.

He's been nothing but cold and rude since you got back to town. There is no level of good looks that can cover up a bad personality.

I tap the glass with my knuckle as I pull the door open. Liam looks over his shoulder without interrupting his taping. "What do you want, Jenna?"

"I just want to talk. You've mastered avoiding me, and you've done a lot of glaring and growling but not a lot of actual talking."

"I don't have anything to say...and I don't growl." I bite on my lower lip, trying not to grin. I don't want to set him off before I get to say my piece, but he definitely does growl.

"I have some things I'd like to say. Can you allow me that, at least?"

His silence is as good an invitation as any. I don't really know where to start, but maybe an apology is the best place. "I'm sorry that I've been insensitive to your grief, Liam. I think that I overlooked how much everything's changed around here, and I want you to know that I'm truly sorry if anything I've said or done since I've been back has hurt or offended you. That's the last thing I would ever want to do. I miss Amy so much, too, but I have no idea what you're going through or what you've been through these past years."

He spins around from where he's been taping the wall, and I almost want to take a step back from the anger that I can see simmering in his eyes. He doesn't raise his voice, but it's almost like he's seething at me, and that's worse, I think. I hear him say, "You're damn right you don't because you weren't here."

I can't tell if he's growling at me again or clenching his teeth to hold back from yelling at me. I need to stay calm, though; I will not bite back.

"Right. I wasn't, and I know things are different now. I shouldn't have expected everything to be the same. I shouldn't have expected to walk back into town and into everyone's welcoming arms without any repercussions for having been gone for six years. But I am back, and I'm not going anywhere. I would love to be your friend again, Liam. I want to at least try to find part of what we used to have. I want a new life in Balsam River with as much of my old life as I can find. I want to leave the city behind me. I want to open a flower shop for our town and add even more beauty to this street and to everyone's lives who walks into my shop. This building is perfect for that. If you can forgive me for my presumptions yesterday, maybe we could discuss some of the details about the shop if you have time." I sigh. "Liam, can we just start over?"

"Start over? Jenna, you don't have the first clue of the effect you have on people in this town. On me. You walk in here like nothing has changed, have a heart-to-heart with my sister and come in here now to apologize to me, and you think that's it? We can go into business now, and life goes on?"

Stay calm. Breathe. Do not raise your voice. He is hurting. You are an outsider to him now. Calm voice.

"Well, yeah, I was kind of hoping." I pause and take a breath. "Liam, I don't know what is going on with you," he scowls and rolls his eyes. He actually rolls his eyes! Are we twelve?

"It's been brought to my attention several times, in fact, that I don't know *you* anymore." I can feel my voice raising despite my best efforts because he is so infuriating.

"But you know what, Liam? That's fine. I don't need to know you; I just need my flower shop. I want to start my life over and make a place for myself in the only place that I feel at home!" My voice is cracking now, all my bravado gone. I don't know if I can convince him. I don't know how to fix this when I don't know what I did wrong.

He's facing me now, and he isn't any less angry. "You're right about one thing: you don't know me, and that's nobody's fault but your own. The years you've missed have turned me into someone you don't know, and you can't take that back. It can't be undone."

"Liam, you have to listen to me when I say that I'm sorry."

"I don't have to do anything you say, you don't even know what you're sorry for. You stand here all high and mighty and think you can just wrap me back around your finger like when we were kids? We were kids, Jenna. There's nothing left of me from that time. You missed the transformation, but this cynical asshole is what's left."

"Liam, don't.... I am sorry! I'm sorry that you've been through hell and back, and I know that I don't know all that you went through. But

I can't help that now, I wasn't even here! What do you want from me?"

The heat coming off him now is palpable. He is so angry and so hurt. Then he lands his killing blow. "That's right, Jenna, you weren't here. You left."

That's it. The look in his eyes tells me everything I need to know. I left him. He needed me. They all did. And I left.

"You and Mark just packed up and left when the times got tough. When we were all going through the hardest days of our entire lives, you two just thought it was a good time to call it quits. Well, we made it through it without you. I know Mark had his own shit; I can't pretend to have any idea what it's like to lose your spouse and with a newborn depending on you on top of that. He had to do what he had to do for himself and for Andria. She needed him more than we needed him."

He runs his hands through his hair. He might be calming down now, but it doesn't even matter. My heart is racing. My face is flushed. My hands are sweating. I can't believe I didn't see this before. I just didn't know it mattered. I didn't know I mattered.

"Liam—"

"No. I'm not done. Do I wish Mark had figured out a way to stay? Of course, I do. I wish we didn't miss those years with Andi, and I wish we could've had each other to lean on. He's my brother. This last year that he's been back has been great. We've worked through some of that stuff, and I can see his side of things. But you? You're different. What did you do? Yeah, you left, but you left for you. No one else."

My stomach drops to my feet as my heart comes up into my throat. I'm dumbfounded. I'm frozen. Say something! But what can I say? He's not wrong. I've ruined everything. I've been ruining everything this whole time, and I had no idea.

CHAPTER

Six

Liam

*I*t feels so good to finally get that all off my chest. To finally tell her how much her actions affected us. Affected me. She was selfish and inconsiderate, and she can't just waltz back in here like nothing happened. She needed to hear this, however harsh it may all sound to her. She acts like everything should be as if she never left. Screw that! She did leave, and who gives a shit that she's back now.

She thinks we can just pick back up where we left off, before my sister had a beautiful baby girl and died before she even got to meet her. Before my best friend got so lost in his own grief that he took off with his daughter to heal somewhere away from the heartbreak. Before she decided she was too good for this town and all of us in it. Before she took her golden-brown eyes and soul-warming smile and ran to the city to live her big city life. Before she broke the little bit of my heart that was left after losing Amy.

I've waited six years to tell her exactly what I think of her and the life she chose to lead instead of staying for the tough times.

Fuck, I remember the day I knew I wasn't worth it to her. The day I knew that she had decided she was done with us. One of the worst days of my life, the day we celebrated the too-short life that my sister had lived.

Standing at the front of this room, like a spectacle for the town to see, really feels like shit.

I hate this. I hate everything. How can she be gone? Why are we up here talking to these people about her in the past tense? How has this become my life?

There are pink roses everywhere, and even more flowers beyond the roses, more than anyone would know what to do with. Amy would love that part, though. She loved flowers. The brighter, the better.

The table to my left is filled with photos of her. Us growing up, her and Mark, their wedding day, a maternity shoot they did last month. Fuck this shit! And fuck Mark too! How dare he just take off? How could he think it would be better for anyone to take Baby Andria and leave? What a piece of shit he turned out to be. My best friend. My brother-in-law. He just left. I've lost my sister, but now my best friend too, and their baby girl with him. Who else can I lose, and how would I ever survive it?

A steady flow of crying faces walks past me, most on their way to my parents. They need this more than I do. Noah seems indifferent, and Sara is focused on holding up Mom. But I just want to get out of here. This event is doing nothing for me but reminding me that I'm alone now.

Then she walks in. Her long brunette hair flows past her shoulders, and her usually golden-brown eyes aren't shining gold today. They look darker than I've ever seen them. She looks paler than the last time I saw her, too. Her eyes are rimmed with red. She's been crying as much as the rest of us. Fuck, I'm a selfish bastard. Jenna lost Amy like the rest of us; she was like a sister to her, and her brother just up and took off with her baby niece, too. I was so consumed by my own grief I haven't reached out to her at all. I don't want her to ever think that she's alone. The rest of the world can fade away and let me down and fucking die too young and break my heart, but I will always have Jenna. I don't care that she's four years younger than me. She turned 18 last month, and I need to tell her how I feel. She won't leave now that we're going through all of this; she can go to school somewhere closer, and we will hold each other together through this bullshit that I am now calling my *life. For the first time since Amy died two weeks ago, I feel a morsel of hope. I feel like maybe there is something else on the other side of this grief. I don't know what it is or what it looks like, but I know that Jenna Davis is there. Our eyes lock, and she looks like she might run into my arms. Yes, run, baby, come let me hold you together too. But then she turns away; she's walking toward Sara; she leans in for a quick hug, says a few words and then follows her mother towards the door.*

She must just be seeing her mom out and then will come to stand with us. She should be here. She's one of us. But she doesn't stop at the door; she keeps going quickly. She's gone. She left.

What was left of my heart cracked into a million pieces. She didn't need me the way I needed her. She didn't care that I was only hanging on by a thread. She would leave, just like Mark, just like Amy. She would leave me like everyone else.

Yeah, I've waited six years, and it does feel good, but it doesn't feel like I thought it would.

The single tear running down Jenna's cheek is really taking the wind out of my confrontational sails. The waterfall of tears that I can tell is about to spill from her eyes isn't helping either. She's wringing her hands together like she's nervous; her eyes are telling me she's genuinely upset about everything I've said, but it can't be coming as a surprise. Can it?

She's the one who left. She did everything I just accused her of. I didn't make any of it up.

She's full-on sobbing now; her face is starting to show red splotches that contrast against her pale cheeks. I can tell that she's struggling to breathe evenly, which makes it seem like she isn't really breathing at all. Maybe that's why the red splotches are so vibrant.

"Shit, Jenna, breathe. Take a deep breath." She gasps, holding her stomach, as she bends over. It sounds like she's trying to catch a breath but can't get air in.

I grab her hand and rub it hard, back and forth between both of mine.

"Jenna, you're okay. Breathe. Please, babe, try to take a deep breath." Her big brown eyes look up at me, still damp with tears but so full of pain and fear. That I put there.

I just unleashed six years of grief, pain and heartache without even thinking of what that would do to her. I am such an asshole. "Jenna, honey, I'm sorry. I shouldn't have said all of that. Not like that. I'm sorry. Breathe in... 1...2...3...4... Now breathe out... 1...2...3...4. Good job, babe, you're doing it. Let's do that again." I hold her hands in both of mine while she breathes in and out until her breathing finally returns to normal.

She takes her hands out of mine and wipes her cheeks. She's staring at me with so much emotion in her eyes that I want to turn away, but something holds me to this spot. I haven't felt anything for her other than disdain for so long; I don't want to feel whatever was buried beneath that. It's been too many years, and I've been hurting for too long.

"Liam."

The way she says my name almost breaks my heart all over again. Fuck this woman and her incredible way of getting under my skin. Her voice cracks with emotion like she might start crying again, and *that* I know I can't handle. Anything but that.

"Jenna. I'm sorry for unleashing all of that on you. It wasn't fair. I couldn't stop once I started. I've wanted to say some of those things to you for six years, but I know now that I didn't actually want to hurt you. I thought that I did. I wanted you to hurt like I did, but I'm so sorry. Please don't cry; I can't stand to be the reason for those tears."

"Liam."

She just says my name with a breath, like she's lost the ability to say more. I shouldn't like how that makes me feel. I shouldn't be thinking of other ways I could have her saying my name breathlessly. God, I am a sick fuck. She's on the tail end of a panic attack, and I'm being a damn pervert. A panic attack I caused because I hate her and her selfish, superficial ways.

Yup, just keep telling yourself that, Liam.

She's still not speaking.

"Jenna, are you okay? I'm gonna need you to say more than just my name."

"I think I'm in shock."

She blinks a few times and uses the back of her hand to wipe her forehead. I don't know if she needs to sit down or what she needs. I glance around the vacant store; there aren't any chairs in here. There's nothing in here except the counter built out from the back wall.

I take her hand again to lead her to the back. "Jenna, come lean on the counter. I don't know what to do to help you. You're scaring me."

"I'm scaring you?" Her voice sounds incredulous now like she might burst into laughter. I'm not even sure if that would be any better than the tears at this point.

Shit, what have I done? She's lost it.

"Jenna, come on. You went from crying to being unable to breathe, and now you're barely speaking, and you kinda look like you might burst out laughing, all in less than ten minutes. What am I supposed to think or do now?"

She leans her elbows on the counter and rests her head on both of her arms. "Liam, you just unleashed a torrent of fury on me that I didn't even know you were capable of feeling, let alone hurling at me. I don't know what to say or do or feel." She yanks her hand from mine. "Can you just give me a minute to process?"

"Yeah...yes.... Jenna, I'm sorry; I know I could have handled that better. It's just that since I saw you walk into my coffee shop two weeks ago, I've felt like I was going to explode, and then you walked in here the next day looking to become my tenant! It felt like I couldn't escape all this pent-up hurt and anger, and if I didn't do something, like get as far away from you as possible or let it out somehow, then I truly would combust. I'm sorry that I upset you, but I'm not sorry for what I said because it's all true."

"Liam, how have you gone from not speaking two words to me for two weeks to not being able to shut up? I need to think! I can't even process all the emotions that I'm feeling right now." She looks up at me and, with so much sadness, says, "You know what? I have to go."

At that, she walks past me and out the door. I'm left standing here looking at her back as she walks away from me without an explanation.

Again.

CHAPTER

Seven

Jenna

What the actual fuck just happened?

I can't catch my breath. Again. My God, Jenna, please don't spiral into another panic attack. Once was bad enough, and of course, Liam had to witness that. But he brought me out of it so quickly. That was weird. Such a contrast to the rest of his behaviour. I hate how my hand felt in his, how his touch stopped the panic before I lost complete control.

Ugh, what a mess.

I'm sitting in my car, pulled over, halfway down the road from my mom's place. I don't know where to go from here. I don't want to explain my current state to anyone, but I can't sit on the side of the road all day. This is why I need my own place, for space.

Apparently, I need space to deal with mental breakdowns after my childhood crush, turned teenage friend, turned mortal enemy, emotionally attacks me on a random Wednesday afternoon.

Fuck my life. How did everything get so messy?

I thought I could stay and talk to Liam once I got my breathing under control, but his hand rubbing mine and his soothing voice trying to calm me was almost worse than feeling his fury. The absolute need to feel his arms around me was all-consuming, and I couldn't even begin to discern what that meant or how either of us would respond to that feeling.

The hurt he was feeling was undeniable, and I couldn't handle standing there looking at him, knowing that I had any part in causing it. I had to get out of there, away from him. I need to figure out how I can fix this. Some of it. Hell, any of it would be a start. He's holding all this resentment towards me because I left town?

I still can't believe that. I never could have imagined that I meant anything more to him than just being another part of our friend group. I spent most of my time with Sara and Amy, or I was just Mark's little sister. How did his kind smile and protective nature translate into my presence, or in this case, my absence, being what broke him after Amy died?

"Jenna, you don't have the first clue of the effect you have on people in this town. On me."

He said on him. I affect him?

Again, what the actual fuck just happened?

"But you, you're different. What did you do? Yeah, you left, but you left for you. No one else."

Tears are pouring down my cheeks at that memory. I rest my head on the top of my steering wheel and just let them fall. Like it's fate, Taylor Swift joins my misery from the radio speakers. At least I can still count on her in my times of need. Listening to her singing Back to December has never sounded so raw.

He tried to give me everything but all I did was say goodbye. Did I even say goodbye? No, I just ran away, and now I can feel my pride slipping away. Damn, she is wise.

I need to go back. I need to tell him why I left, that I didn't know he needed me. I didn't know anyone did. How did I completely miss everything he was thinking and feeling back then?

If I'm honest with myself, I went from having a crazy childhood crush on Liam to genuinely feeling like I was in love with him when I was in high school to needing nothing more than to be away from all of them.

When Amy died, it felt like everything that was good and pure and made sense in life was just gone. I didn't just turn off my feelings, but everyone's world was literally flipped upside down. Mark's most of all, but the Ryan's were going through something that I just couldn't relate to or help them with. I felt like their grief trumped mine, and then I felt so much guilt for feeling my own grief at all. I couldn't help but minimize my pain in their presence, and I got tired of doing that. I needed to get away from here so that I could feel my feelings. When Mark left, I felt so alone.

Looking back now, I think I got lost in that grief and loneliness. I had lost my sister-in-law, who was also one of my best friends, and then, within two weeks of that, it felt like I lost my brother and my brand-new niece, too. I needed to grieve, and I just didn't know how to do that next to them.

Now I'm wondering if those choices six years ago have cost me everything that I thought I had left. This town, my friends, Mark and Mom, those are the things I came back for. I know Mark and Mom will always have my back, but everything else that I was missing in Toronto is here, or so I thought. What if I lost them a long time ago without even realizing it?

I just want to scream and cry and hit something. I smack my hand hard on my steering wheel with a loud guttural scream that makes me feel like I've done something useful. I wince as I rub my palm, damn it, now my hand is sore. Nice going, Jenna! I shriek as something...or someone, rather, taps on my window.

Liam?

CHAPTER

Liam

I'm driving down the same dirt road I've driven down for my entire life to get to my house. I just passed the driveway to the one I grew up in, and I can almost see my own house that I built about five years back. I really love my little corner of paradise on the southwest edge of my family's farm. I built a modest bungalow, designed it myself and really made it my own. I didn't know how much I needed my own space until I got it.

Shit, am I ever feeling that today? I can't wait to get home and untangle this terrible day from my soul. An ice-cold beer will most definitely help with that process. I'm just a couple kilometres from my place when I notice a blue Corolla pulled over on the side of the road. The same blue Corolla I've been avoiding for two weeks.

A lot of good that did me anyway.

What is Jenna doing sitting out here? Why wouldn't she have gone home after she left me standing alone and dumbfounded in my vacant building? She must be having car trouble. She's probably the last person I want to see right now, but there's no way I'm leaving her stranded out here. Stranded might be an overstatement; her mother's place is only half a kilometre past mine. If her car was acting up, I'm sure she would have just left it and walked. My stomach clenches at the thought that there's something else wrong. Maybe she's hurt in some way.

I throw my truck in park and rush over to her driver's door to make sure she's okay. I can see instantly that she's been crying again; her eyes are red and puffy, and her cheeks are still glistening with tears. I try to contain my wince as I think of Jenna hurting; even if it's an emotional pain, it physically hurts me to think I caused any of it. My stomach lurches as I notice *her* wincing and rubbing the palm of her hand. She is hurt. Fuck. What happened between the time she left me twenty minutes ago and right now?

I tap on her window to get her attention. I need her out of the car; I need to know what happened and that she's okay. She jumps and screams at the sound of my knuckle on the glass right next to her head. On any other day, I would've laughed at her shriek, but today, I just need to touch her and know that she's not hurt badly.

I throw open her door. "Jenna! What are you doing sitting on the side of the road? Where are you hurt?" I can't slow down my thoughts and my panic. Why does she always make me feel so out of control?

"Liam, what the fuck? You scared the shit out of me!"

"What the fuck yourself. I'm on my way home and saw your car on the side of the road. You've clearly been crying, and you're holding your hand in pain. What happened?"

"You know what? I'm really getting tired of your hot and cold, macho man attitude! What is it to you where I park my car or what I'm doing in it?"

This woman...will be the end of me.

"Listen, you better drop the 'I'm an independent business woman from the city' act and get used to the worry and safety that comes with being back in your hometown. I wanted to make sure you're okay. Clearly, you are. Have a nice night."

I can't handle this back and forth with her. She says I'm hot and cold. I get an ice queen one minute and a sweet, apologetic hometown girl the next. I don't know what to do with her. I feel like I can't talk to her anymore. I'm so used to being consumed by rage and hurt that I don't know how to feel now that I've let that all out.

I need to get home, take a hot shower and give her some space to process, like she asked. I turn to walk away, but before I take another step, I feel her warm fingers wrap around my wrist. After all these years, it still feels like her hand belongs on my arm, or wrapped in my own, or running through my hair when it's just a little too long... Ugh, stop that thought right there. Not going there.

I glance down at it, then back up to her eyes. She's still seated in her car, but the fading sunlight from the sky is making her brown eyes shine brighter than I've seen them in years. The red rimming them does nothing to deter me from all the shades of gold, brown and hazel that she's holding my attention with.

Her voice cracks with emotion. "Liam, wait."

That plea, combined with her hand grasping my wrist tighter, stops me in my tracks.

"What, Jenna? Wait for what?"

She exhales a loud sigh. "I want to talk to you. I'm sorry for snapping at you. Thank you for stopping to check on me. I am fine, though. I was upset and didn't want to go home, in case... I didn't want my mom to see me like this. I got a little worked up, smacked my steering wheel and hurt my hand. I'm sorry to have worried you. I was just about to leave, though; I was coming to find you."

Coming to find me? That would be a first for her, coming back after she leaves me staring at her back.

"Well, here I am. What more could we possibly have to say?"

"Can we go somewhere to talk? Somewhere that isn't the side of the road?"

"Jenna, is that a good idea? Didn't we just try that? I think it ended badly, and you said you needed time to think." She's standing now, staring into my eyes, like she can make a point with just one look. I forgot how short she is, maybe five foot three inches, but I tower at least a foot over her, and despite this crazy day, that look makes me want to wrap her up in my long arms and never let her go. She used to fit in them so perfectly.

"I have been sitting here thinking, and I've pretty much had enough of it. It's not getting me anywhere. I need to tell you my side of our past. I want to tell you what's in my heart. I don't want to fight with you anymore. If you will listen to me, then I will listen to you after I've said my piece. We're grown-ass adults and should be able to sit down together and work this out. Fuck Liam, you used to be one of my best friends. Can we not at least remember that for a moment? We can give this," she waves her other hand between us, "give us the time and consideration that it deserves."

How could she think that I've forgotten I was one of her best friends? She was mine, too. She was everything. She's right, though. We do owe each other at least this much. "Okay, let's just pull up into my place here; we can sit on the porch and talk," I point ahead to where my property starts. My driveway is a little way up the road. I just hope I don't regret letting her in. I don't want to find out if there's anything left of my heart that's not yet broken.

CHAPTER

Nine

Liam

I step into my house to grab a blanket for Jenna. I feel like outside is a safer space for this conversation, but the sun is sinking, and I don't want her to be cold. A better man would just welcome her inside, but I don't think I can add the image of her to the interior of my home. I designed it all myself, and it's everything I've ever wanted, as far as the bones and look of my dream house go. Of course, there is still a blank space where the woman I will marry someday belongs and the family we will raise together. I'm determined to keep that space blank in my mind so as not to feed into any preconceived notions that I once had of that woman being Jenna.

So, yeah, it's definitely much better if she stays outside. "Here," I pass her the blanket as she lowers herself into the wooden rocker at the far end of the porch. There's another rocking chair beside her with a small table sitting between them. I decide to sit in the other one, avoiding the porch swing that sits closer to the door. She probably avoided it on purpose, too. It's the same one we used to all cram onto as kids when it was hanging on my parents' porch.

Memories. They'll get ya every damn time. Yup, definitely keeping this conversation outdoors. She's wringing her hands together again; she's nervous. Again.

I want to hold them still. I want to ease her nerves and her pain. Whatever I said that has her so torn up, I want to unsay it. Why did I think I needed to unleash that all on her? To make myself feel better? Nice fucking job, Liam, selfish prick.

She looks up from where she was staring at her hands; she locks eyes with me. I don't know what she wants me to do or say. She's the one who wanted to talk, and I was ready to give her the space she asked for.

She must realize this too because she looks down again and says, "I don't know where to start, Liam. I think so much of this hurt and confusion goes back to before Amy died. I don't want to hurt you more by bringing that up, but I don't know how else to understand or how to make you understand."

My jaw clenches, and her eyes go right to the spot where I know my muscle is twitching on the side of my face. "See, I've already made you angry." She goes to stand up, "This was a bad idea."

I can't let this end this way again. We have to push through the pain and discomfort at some point, so it might as well be now, "No, Jenna. You're right. It does hurt, but I'm not angry, not that you want to talk about it anyway. I have been angry for so many years, at you, at Mark, at God, at Amy, anything or anyone that ever left or caused someone to leave. But sitting here with you, seeing you trying, and seeing how nervous and upset this makes you too, I'm not angry, Jenna, I'm just scared. I'm scared to feel anything else. It's been so long since I've felt anything. I've just been numb this whole time until you moved back. I'm scared that this won't solve anything, that we'll leave this porch more scarred than when we stepped onto it. But I want to hear what you have to say. I want to try to understand, too."

She takes a deep breath and tells me everything. How she had the biggest crush on me since she was ten years old, that in high school, when we all included her in our stupid adventures and when I always stuck up for her and stood by her, it made her feel safe and accepted.

I can't help but smirk. The crap we got up to in those days usually was stupid, but being there for her was everything to me; that's exactly what I wanted to do; make her feel safe.

She tells me that as the years went on, she thought that she'd fallen in love with me, but she knew it was unrequited, and she knew because I was four years older, I would never look at her that way.

Damn, this girl has no idea.

Wait. What? She had no idea? What the fuck?

"Jenna! Stop. What are you talking about?"

"I'm trying to explain to you what it was like for me. As you guys all grew up, you left me behind. I get it! I really do. I wasn't mad, and I'm still not, but it was hard being so much younger and trying to find my place in the world of high school drama and university admissions without you guys by my side. Then everything, well... you know, everything with Amy was just too hard. For all of us. I know it wasn't the same for me as it was for you---"

"Okay, that's enough. I don't know what fucked up story you've been telling yourself all these years, but no one left you behind, and it *was* the same for you when Amy died. Amy died! That doesn't play out differently, no matter how you say it. It was fucking awful, it still is fucking awful, but it happened... to all of us."

"Liam, I know, but she was your *sister!* That is not the same as who she was to me; she was a lot to me, but she was everything to you."

"You don't get it. You can't compare grief. It took me a long time to realize this, but what hurt me also hurt you, and Mark, and Andi, and Mom and Dad, and Paul at the pizza shop. We all loved her, and we all miss her. Yes, it affects us differently. Everyone's relationships were different. But did Mark love her more than I did? Fuck no! Is the loss of her different for him than it is for me? Fuckin' right it is. She wasn't my wife or daughter, just like she wasn't your sister, but we all *lost* her. Every single one of us."

Her eyes fill with tears, and they run down her cheeks. I lift my hand to wipe them away, but I stop myself. I still don't know what she's thinking or why she thinks this is an argument for why she left. Sounds like shit got hard, and she bailed. Just like I thought.

She watches me lower my hand back to rest on my leg, and I swear I see her flinch.

"I don't think I was capable of understanding any of that at the time. Honestly, I don't know if I am capable now. I felt like an outsider looking in on your family falling apart. It felt like if I fell apart at your feet, I would just be adding more weight to your already unimaginable burden. You rallied with your brother, sister and parents—and so you should have. I'm not suggesting otherwise, but then Mark left with Baby Andi, and I was so alone. I was so fucking sad and so scared of facing life without her. I just finished my enrolment to U of T and booked it to the city as fast as I could."

She puts her face in her hands; she's crying softly, then looks up, and through broken sobs, she says, "I never, in a million years, was leaving to 'leave you,' I was not abandoning you, not in my head anyway, in my head you didn't need me. You'd already left me behind. I just needed space to breathe, to grieve away from here. I can see now, after listening to you earlier, that I was wrong, that I was weak, and that I should have pushed my way in. But Liam, I don't know if I could've handled any more heartbreak. I didn't know how any of you would respond to that. I can't honestly say if I could go back if I would do anything differently. I did what I had to do for me, and if that makes me a selfish bitch, then I guess I am. I'm so sorry for the pain that caused you, though. If I had known what you needed, I definitely would have done things differently. But, I just didn't know."

I reach to brush her tears off her cheeks now. I can't help it. I need to touch her, to soothe her hurt in some way. I wish my thumb wiping a tear could wipe away all the pain that's shining in her eyes. I can't believe she didn't know.

Fuck me, she didn't know.

I can't form the words that I need to right now. "Jenna" is all I get out before I kneel in front of her and wrap my arms around her. I hold onto her so tightly, as if she might somehow get away again like this might be the only chance I get.

I have to make her understand how much her leaving broke me, how much I've loved her since before I knew what love was.

She's sobbing into my chest, and I can't imagine being anywhere else but here at this moment. I rest my hand gently on the back of her head, her hair so smooth beneath my fingers. I use my other hand to rub small circles in the center of her back.

"Jenna, babe, don't cry. It's okay. It's going to be okay; I promise you." She lifts her head to look at me. Reluctantly, I let my hand fall from her hair; I rest it on her forearm as she says, "How can you say that? You hate me. I've ruined one of the only good things that I had left in this world. Nothing else matters in this town if I don't have your friendship."

"I'm right here, and we're going to work this out. I understand now, and I want to explain myself better than I did earlier today at the shop, I mean without yelling and swearing at you." She almost grins at that, and the twist in my stomach lets go just a little bit. "I want you to know where I was coming from, but I'm not going to say it's going to make any sense, not anymore. And I'm so sorry for that."

"Liam, what do you mean? You said that I left, and you'll never forgive me for that. You're right, I did."

"Ya, I did say that, and I was being a selfish asshole. I think maybe I've been a selfish asshole for the past six years. I'm not too sure, though." I smirk, hoping she can feel lighter at my self-deprecating tone.

"No! You were hurting. You were grieving. We can't change what grief does to us. The way it makes us think, feel, and act is so far beyond our control at the time when we're in the trenches. It evokes an instinctual reaction, physically and emotionally, and all we can do is show grace to ourselves and others who are experiencing it. There will be regrets as you come out of the fog, but it could take months or years for that to happen. Don't ever let those regrets turn into guilt; they are not the same thing. You can wish things didn't happen the way they did and still hold an understanding that it wasn't your fault that they did, in fact, happen that way."

"You're right, but I want you to know that that's exactly what happened. I wasn't thinking of you or your grief. All I could think about was myself and my family. Nothing else mattered. I don't think that's the way it should've been, but I can't change that's how it was. I needed you. I wanted you to be there, to hold me and make it, even, just a little bit better, but I didn't tell you that. I wanted you to just know, and that's not fair."

Her fingers are rubbing my knuckles softly, "I'm so sorry I didn't know, though." Tears overflow from her eyes again.

"I'm sorry, too. You're not wrong when you say Amy's death changed everything. I didn't know I pulled back from you before that, but now that you explain your side of things, I guess I did, but it wasn't to leave you behind or because you weren't important, Jenna; it was the opposite. I was waiting for you."

"Waiting for me? For what?"

"Waiting for you to graduate, waiting for you to be eighteen. I was waiting to tell you everything I've felt for you since we were kids. Everything got stronger and more intense as we grew up, but Jenna, I was twenty-one, almost twenty-two. I couldn't move forward with you until you graduated. Our parents would have flipped. Maybe I should have said something anyways, and we could've figured it out in the meantime, but I don't think I could have stayed away if my feelings were out in the open."

"Stayed away? You were staying away?" Her eyes widen as the realization hits her. That this is why we weren't as close that last year before everything with Amy.

"I had to!" I run my hands through my hair like that can turn back time. "I had to," I say softer this time. "I couldn't stand to be near you and not have you. I couldn't stand to touch you but not hold you or kiss you. You were mine, in my head at least; there was never anyone else for me, but you were still so young, and Mark and Amy were getting married, and I didn't want to cause drama to ruin any of that for anyone."

"Liam. I loved you then. I would've done anything if I had known. I would've fallen off my chair and likely gone to the hospital for a concussion check, but I would have done anything, I would have understood, I would have waited."

She loved me then. Past tense. I've royally fucked this up.

"I don't know, I'm really not sure if I did the right or wrong thing after Amy died. I know I should have spoken up. I should have told you everything. I'm so sorry that I didn't. I was just so lost and broken. But even before that, I don't know if it would've worked out. I was too nervous and felt too guilty for all my feelings. I can't change it now anyway. All I can do is ask for your forgiveness."

"Why didn't you tell me after Amy? I didn't leave right away; Mark did, but I was in town for two months after."

All I can do is shake my head. Remembering those two months is like feeling knives stabbing through my chest. My fists clench, and my jaw tightens. I can't believe that six years later, the memories still cause such a physical reaction. "You left me before you left town, Jenna."

"What do you mean? I was right here."

"You came to the celebration of life with your mom. You looked me right in the eyes and turned away. You spoke with Sara, and then.... You left."

Her cheeks flush red, "No. Liam, I didn't know what else to do! I was on the outside looking in and all alone, to boot. Mark had left, Amy was gone, and we were all broken, but my pieces didn't fit in with yours."

"But they did, Jenna. They could have. I have never felt as alone as I did that day when you turned your back on me." I can't stop the tingle from behind my eyes. I haven't cried over this in six years, but I can almost feel what it felt like that day when I thought she didn't care.

"I know now that's not what you were doing. But do you see now, there's no way I could tell you how much I loved you, that I wanted a life with you. I thought you didn't care and that you had given up, that you wanted to live your life away from Balsam River, away from the pain and memories, and away from me."

She whispers, "Oh, Liam," and reaches for me now. Her arms are around my neck. Her lips crash into mine. My hands instinctively go to hold her face as her fingers drag through my hair. I've longed for this kiss for most of my adult life, shit, even before I was an adult.

Even when I thought I hated her, I didn't; I've always loved her. I hated that she left, that she wasn't here with me, but I could never hate *her.*

CHAPTER

Ten

Jenna

Liam's rough, callused hands against my cheeks are enough to set my soul on fire. His tongue tangles with mine like we've done this a thousand times. I can't help the soft noise that escapes my throat. I think that's what joy must sound like. I can't believe how right this feels. How could I have been missing this my entire life? It's like the 24 years I've lived were all just to get me to this place, in this moment, with Liam in my arms. He pulls away slowly.

Ugh, no, don't. I'm not ready for this to end. Looking into his eyes, I notice they're back to the bright, sparkling blue that I remember. How could one afternoon have erased so much darkness?

"Liam, don't stop. Don't tell me you can't, or that you won't, or that we shouldn't. Please don't take this moment from me."

He barks out a laugh, a loud "Ha!" then leans in and places the softest kiss on my lips, so lightly that I can barely feel it. "Nothing could keep me from you, my love. Now that you're back, now that you're here, on my porch, in my arms, you're never leaving. I knew it would be like this. If you could ever love me back, I knew it would be this perfect."

"I never stopped loving you; I just stopped listening to my heart." He takes my hand and leads me down the porch to the swing that's hanging next to his front door.

"Is that..." He smiles knowingly. "Yup, one and the same."

"Wow. I can't believe it's still around. We had so many good times sitting on this swing. Remember when we all used to fit on it?" I laugh lightly, remembering our childhood. So many shared memories that turned into so many shared heartaches.

He's moving his thumb back and forth on the top of my hand so gently. "We can have more good times here, Jenna. Everything's going to be different now."

"Does this mean I get my flower shop?" I'm being cheeky, but I can't help it. His answering smile tells me it wasn't too soon. Thank God.

"You can have anything you want, my Jenny girl."

My Jenny girl.

Is this real? Is this really happening right now? We sit on the swing side by side. I lean into him just to see what it feels like to be close to him again. He swings his arm around my shoulders and plays with the ends of my hair while he leans down and places his lips on the top of my head.

I feel his lips curve into a smile against my hair. "This is real, and it is really happening."

Shit, did I say that out loud?

I feel like I'm walking through a dream. This is a dream that I've had a thousand times before, where I come home, and Liam welcomes me back into his life with open arms, professing his love for me. That was laughable this morning when I thought he hated me.

"I feel like I don't even know you anymore."

He jerks away quickly, causing me to almost fall over on the narrow swing. "What do you mean?" His voice sounds strained like he's about to panic. I rest my hand on his thigh. "Just wait, don't freak out. I just mean, so much time has passed. I was a kid the last time we spoke more than ten words to each other, and I know the last six years have changed you.

You told me yourself that I have no idea who you are anymore. I want to get to know you again. I want to know the Liam that you are now. Tell me everything I missed."

"I thought you were suggesting this wouldn't work because you don't know me anymore. Don't ever think that so much has changed that I won't walk through fire for you."

I lean over and kiss his cheek. "I know. I didn't mean that at all. I just don't want to rush into this blindly. We have to take the time we need to heal and get reacquainted and just be together, with no hurts and no more miscommunication getting in the way."

He squeezes my hand tightly. "Yes. Yes, a hundred times, I want that too. I want to know the beautiful, amazing woman that you've turned into. Tell me why you came back home. Tell me everything about living in the city, your job, your friends; I want to know everything."

I can't help but laugh because he has no idea. "Liam, the city sucked. It was loud and dirty and too crowded. I was surrounded by people 24/7 while feeling lonelier than I've ever felt in my life. My apartment was a one-room studio that cost me almost half of my salary each month. I didn't have any close friends. I went out with some girls from work from time to time, but I mostly just worked and spent time at home reading and catching up with my mom and Mark. I know some people love the hustle and bustle and having so many resources at their fingertips, but that's just not me. It never was. I needed to go because I wanted my degree from the best business school in Ontario. I stayed to make enough money to save up, and to get experience in business, to be confident in my knowledge and abilities so that I could open my own business back here one day and not worry that I wasn't good enough." He's looking at me wide-eyed now, like he can't believe anything I'm saying.

"I know, sad, right? But that's the truth. Not much has changed for me. My whole reason for coming back was to make the change happen! I want to open my own flower shop; I want to be a businesswoman in this beautiful town that has always been home to me. I want to join the 'Women in Business of Balsam River's Facebook group and teach them all the little things I've learned over the years that will make us all more successful. I want to find a cute little house on a back road somewhere. One with enough property to have gardens like my mom's and enough bedrooms that Andi can come have sleepovers. I want to have wine nights with Sara. Oooh! And I'd love to invite Sherri now too, do you know how great she is? You did good with that one!" I wave my hand between us because I'm rambling again and need to stop. "Anyways, I want all of that, and now... I want you. I want to sit on this porch together with steaming cups of coffee. I want your arms wrapped around me, and I want everything that I thought I would never have."

The look he's giving me now is so tender I could just melt. His feelings are always written plain as day across his face, and I've never been so grateful for that as I am right now. Love is pouring from his eyes and falling straight into my wounded heart, healing every crack and chip that was ever made. "What are you smiling about?" I ask him.

"Is it bad that I'm glad you hated the city?" I smack his chest. "Yes, that is bad! You're happy that I was miserable for the last six years?"

"Well, if it brought you back here." His mouth lifts on one side into his signature crooked smile but then lowers again as his eyes turn serious. "I'm sorry you weren't happy, but I'm also glad that you reached your goals. I'm so proud of you, Jenny girl." He reaches for my chin, holding it between his thumb and forefinger. "You didn't let anything hold you back. You plowed through your grief and did what you'd always planned. Amy would be so proud, too."

Hearing him say that he's proud of me, that he's not holding these years we've missed against me, makes me feel things I've never felt before. I don't know how to put words to what he's doing to me. I want to tell him, but I think the only way he'll understand is if I show him. Without letting go of his hand, I stand up and sit back down on his lap. He smiles, looking back and forth between my eyes, trying to guess what I'll do next. I run both my hands up his chest, and I can tell he's no longer the scrawny teenage boy I fell in love with. As I slide my hands around behind his neck and into his hair, the deep guttural groan that escapes his lips as I massage his scalp with my fingertips makes my whole body warm with want.

"I look at you in front of me right now, and I think I must be dreaming."

"Funny, I was just thinking the same thing." I lean in and place my lips against his. His tongue teases my lips open and searches for mine like he's been searching for me all these years. I can feel his love and passion run through my whole body. His hands roam across my back and into my hair. I feel him everywhere, but it's not enough. I want more. I want everything he has to give. I swear to myself, right now, nothing will ever keep us apart again. I don't care that I don't know the man he's grown into. I will love every part of him, every version.

He's Liam, my best friend, my love.

CHAPTER

Eleven

Jenna

I don't want to move, and I definitely don't want to leave. We eventually made our way inside the house, which is beautiful, by the way! The whole thing is open concept, with vaulted ceilings, old barn beams running across a sunken living room, with the coziest couch that I happen to find myself snuggled on right now. The living room faces the east with a wall of windows, perfect to watch the sunrise. It's like he built the house in the perfect position for that and to watch the sunsets out on the porch. The kitchen isn't super fancy, but it matches the house perfectly. It's a large open space with a huge island in the middle and three walls surrounding it, lined with appliances and natural walnut cabinets. God, it's beautiful. This whole place feels like an old farmhouse, except it's all brand new.

We've been snuggled here for hours, just talking and catching up and then sitting in silence for a while. I've been basking in his warmth and scent that is that oh-so-masculine and country boy-esque, pretty much everything that I've been missing for six years. I start to unwrap myself from the cocoon that Liam has me in and tilt my head up and to the side to see if he's awake. Oh, he's awake, just staring at me like a creeper.

"Can I help you?"

He laughs a deep, rumbly laugh that makes my stomach take flight with butterflies. "If you're offering…"

"Ha-ha, very funny. I was actually thinking that I should get going. I texted Mom that I would be late getting home, but I do have to go home at some point." Ugh, I almost forgot that I have to go home and face my mother. How do I even begin to explain everything that happened today? Was it only this morning that I sat and chatted with Sherri about trying to work things out with Liam? She will get a kick out of this development! I actually can't wait to tell her all about this. My mother, on the other hand, I'm not sure how she'll take it. She's a little possessive of me since I've been back, and I don't know if she'll take issue with our history. The age difference doesn't matter now like it would've as teens, but I don't know if she knows that we aren't teens anymore.

Liam groans as he stretches and sits up on the couch. "I guess I can release you. If I must." He winks at me, and… yup, there goes my butterflies again. "When can I see you again?" he asks quietly. I love how eager he is for us to be together. It's everything that I need.

"Tomorrow? Coffee at Liam's happens to be the most important part of my morning routine."

He chuckles and pokes me in the ribs. "Don't get cheeky with me. I don't want to let you go at all, but yeah, I guess tomorrow will be okay." His smile brightens up the entire room.

"I've never felt so light and complete, Jenna. This is it for me. You are it. I know that sounds like a lot right now, and the last thing I want to do is scare you. But I need you to know that I'm serious. I'm not going to hide this… I'm not going to hide *us*. I'm going to grab you and kiss you tomorrow morning as soon as you set foot in my coffee shop. You will have breakfast with me before your visit with Sherri because I know I can't monopolize your entire day. Pat on the back for me, thank you." He mimics patting himself on the shoulder. What a dork.

"But I need you to know that we're together. I love you, Jenna, and you are finally mine." He grabs both of my hands and flips them over; he places a soft kiss on each palm, then leans in and kisses my forehead.

Yes, he is, for real, this perfect.

"I know Liam, and I love you too. Everything you just said is like you're reading my heart. I am a little worried about what my mom will say, and.... Oh my God, Liam! I just realized we have to tell Mark! Is he going to be okay with this? You guys are just gaining your friendship and trust back. I don't want to stand in the way of any of that."

"It's okay, babe, he'll be fine. Trust me." I want to trust him, but I know my brother, and even though we've lived in different cities for the last six years, he's fiercely protective of me. Despite him leaving town after Amy's death, he never lost touch with me, like he did the rest of the town. He never stopped worrying and checking in with how I was doing, who I was seeing, protecting my heart, even if I wasn't. If anything, that all got worse after Amy died. It was like because he failed at protecting her, he needed to protect me tenfold.

I explain this to Liam, and he just smiles. "I know, I get that. I think that's another reason it killed me when you left back then. I just wanted to keep everyone close and safe, and I couldn't reach you. I was so afraid that something was going to happen to you, that you'd get in an accident in the city or into a bad relationship, and no one would ever know. I felt like I failed Amy too, and Andi and Mark, if I'm honest, carried around a lot of guilt for a long time that I failed everyone. Logically, I know there's nothing anyone could have done. It was just a freak occurrence. There are risks in everything we do, and having a baby can go wonderfully perfect or horribly wrong. I think we just never thought it would happen to us. I definitely failed to see your pain, and I won't make that mistake again. We'll sit down and talk to Mark together. He will understand that life is too fragile to miss out on a love like this. I won't let anything stand in my way anyways, so he won't have much of a choice."

That makes me laugh. I don't know if it'll be as easy as he thinks, but I'm willing to find out.

"Okay, I gotta go," I lean down to his spot on the couch and give him a quick kiss. "I will see you in the morning. I love you."

"I love you too, babe, so much."

This is so weird. Liam Ryan loves me.

Gosh, it feels like this moved fast! I know it did, but it feels so natural to finally be able to tell him that I love him. After so many years of hiding it, being able to say it out loud feels like a weight lifted off my shoulders, like my heart is finally free to feel.

"Okay, what happened? Who has put that beautiful smile back on your face?" My cheeks heat as my mother glares at me with a twinkle in her eye. How do moms always know?

"Well, you're taking the fun out of it by calling me out, Mom. If you must know, I was going to sit down and tell you that I've had a crazy afternoon and evening.... with Liam."

"With Liam! Liam Ryan?"

"Yes, Ma, how many Liams do you know?"

"A civil afternoon and evening? Wait, why afternoon *and* evening? What's going on?"

"Yes. We talked. No yelling, no storming out. Well, there was all that at first, but then we talked minus the theatrics. It was so good, Mom. He listened, and I needed to do my part and listen to him, too. We had everything all wrong. It turns out... he was in love with me back before I left for school." I pause for her to react but then continue, "I really hurt him by leaving, and he's been so rude and nasty to me since I've been back as a result of that pain." I wait for her shrieks or cries or clapping... something. Anything. This silence and 'so what?' look on her face really isn't doing it for me.

"Aren't you going to say something?" She bursts out laughing. She's laughing? Why is she laughing? This isn't even remotely funny in any way. I'm so confused right now. She must notice the look on my face because, through gasping breaths, she says, "Oh, honey, I'm sorry!" She's sorry, but she can't control her laughter long enough to explain what the heck her problem is.

"I'm so sorry." She's still trying to catch her breath enough to speak, holding her chest, she finally calms enough. "You didn't know that Liam Ryan was in love with you?"

"What?" I'm the one shrieking now. "What do you mean, I didn't know? You did?"

"Oh, sweetie, everyone did. That boy doted on you like you were the princess of the town. He loved you before he knew what real love was."

"Oh my God, Mom! I don't understand how you know this."

"Well, dear, it was just so obvious."

"Why didn't you say anything to me?" I need to sit down. I can't believe my mother has had more knowledge this whole time about my love life, or lack thereof than I did.

"Oh..." She looks sad now but continues, "I didn't think it was my place. No one ever knows what to do for the grieving. It's hard enough when you're on the outside, but it's even harder, when you're also grieving, just on another level. We were all so broken after Amy. And then Mark needed his space, and you followed suit. I didn't know anymore where anyone's heart was at. It wasn't my place, Honey, please understand that."

"I do, Mom; you're right, it was too hard."

"Whenever you came back to visit, you kept your distance from all the Ryans, so I just assumed it hurt more than it helped to be with them. Love can't withstand some hurts, you know; I just thought this one was too big for such a young love."

"You know, Ma, maybe it was. Maybe we needed to be apart to be able to come back together like we have. Our puzzle isn't broken. When someone you love dies, their piece is missing, and that will always hurt like hell, but we are still here, and we are still connected in all the ways that we always were."

She's crying now, and I can't stop my own tears from joining hers. I move in and wrap my arms around her; she's the perfect height for me to still rest my head on her shoulder. "I hope you've worked it all out now, darling; that boy is only half of himself without you."

"We have, Mom, thanks. I think I was walking around without half of my heart all these years, too."

"Ah yes, it's all going to be okay, Jenna."

"I think so too, Mom."

"Holy shit girl, what was that?"

Sherri just witnessed the aforementioned 'kiss as soon as I walked into Liam's,' she's a little confused and a lot excited. A lot can change in eighteen hours.

"Um, so... we worked things out."

"Ha! I noticed. Tell. Me. Everything."

I'm as giddy as she is. I feel like I'm in high school again, except this time, I got the guy. "I will, I will, I promise. I told Liam we could have breakfast together first, but as soon as we're done, he promised he would cover for you if he had to, so we can hide away and catch up."

She rolls her eyes as Liam wraps his arm around my waist. "Breakfast, Jenna?" He's trying not to be rude but can't even contain his excitement that I'm here, with him, for breakfast together. I know the feeling. I smile back at Sherri over my shoulder as we walk to the back corner table where Sherri and I usually sit. Liam rests his hand on the small of my back as he guides me to my chair. The warmth from his hand sends my stomach aflutter and has my cheeks reddening. Just a simple touch from him can make me feel things I've never felt before, at least not for a very long time, when brushes of his fingers or friendly hugs and nudges used to do the same things to me.

I am officially a loser. Crushing this hard on my childhood best friend turned boyfriend. Oh my God. Liam is my boyfriend. As much as I want to jump up and down and squeal like I'm in high school again, my boyfriend sounds so juvenile for what he is to me. What we have is so much more. There's nothing else to call it, but it just doesn't feel like enough. It feels like everything, against all odds, is finally coming together. Like now, and not a moment before, I am home.

After we've finished eating and talking about everything and nothing at the same time, Sherri is hovering just out of hearing range, waiting for her turn. I laugh and tell Liam, "We better say goodbye; Sherri needs her intel. You must have work to do. It's nearly 9... oh no, I'm so sorry, have I kept you from things?"

His chuckle warms my insides as he says, "Never. Work keeps me from some things, but you will always be the priority. I guess I can concede some of my Jenna time for Sherri to get her fix."

His eyes are shining so bright as he laughs and waves Sherri over. I can almost forget how dark they've been these last couple of weeks; it makes me feel so good to know that he's as happy as I am right now.

He stands for what I think will be a quick hug and a peck on the cheek before he heads to his office, but in fact, it ends up being a passionate embrace and a kiss to forget all other kisses. As his hands roam slightly lower than is appropriate for a public place, I can't help but get lost in him. The taste of coffee and maple syrup melted with the scent of his Old Spice is having me come undone in the middle of a damn coffee shop. It's like no one else is around. His kiss has sucked me into a vortex where it's just him and I and----

"What the fuck is going on here?" My brother's angry voice, coming from the entrance to the shop behind Liam, shatters all dreams of kisses and Old Spice vortexes. "Shit," Liam whispers against my lips. The urge I have to burst out laughing is highly unexpected, not to mention inappropriate for this situation, but I can't deny that the urge is present. Willing myself not to start convulsing with uncontrollable laughter, I slowly step away from Liam. He grabs my hand and just as slowly turns around to face my brother. We are both acting like if we move too quickly, we might detonate a bomb. That thought makes me want to laugh again. What is wrong with me? Be serious, Jenna, this is serious stuff; by the sound of Mark's voice, he very well could explode like a bomb.

I try gently first. "Mark before you freak out---"

"Before I freak out, Jenna? Oh, I'm freaking out, do you know what I just witnessed?" His eyes drop to our hands joined between us, then shoot back up, straight to Liam, then to me, then back to Liam.

"And I repeat, what the fuck is going on here?"

Liam's turn. "Mark, brother, come on, we can talk about this like—"

"Stop right there. Brother? My brother kissing my sister? Sounds like all kinds of fucked up to me, man. If you can even call that kissing, I don't know what the fuck that was. Didn't seem like something your patrons would want to witness. If you're my brother, is Jenna not like a sister to you?"

Liam's body tenses. "Okay, no. Don't even. She has never been like a sister to me, and if you can't see that, then you need to get your head out of your own ass. Can we please take this to my office, so we don't cause a scene?"

"A scene? Like the one you were just causing with your tongue down my sister's throat? Argh! What the fuck, man?" Then, from behind Mark, we hear, "Mark! Office. Now!"

Whoa! That was Sherri; not sure where she came from, but her tone brooked no argument. Mark heads to the hallway that leads to Liam's office. Hmm, that's weird. Mark doesn't follow directions from anybody.

Anybody except Sherri, apparently. He glares at her as he passes where she's moved to be standing behind the counter. Okay, so he's not following her direction happily, but still. Thank God Andi isn't here; he must have just come from dropping her at school, small blessings. Liam closes the door behind me as Mark spins around to look at us both again. Liam still hasn't let go of my hand. I guess he's proving a point. "Someone want to tell me what this is?" Mark waves his hand furiously toward us and our joined hands.

Liam starts to speak, but I cut him off by saying, "Liam and I are together." I wasn't sure what the best way to do this was, but now that we're here, I'm going with the 'ripping off the band-aid' method.

"You're who and the what now?" His quirky way of working through problems he can't solve makes me smile. He'll be okay with this once he works through it in his head. He loves us both. It'll be okay. It has to be.

"Liam and I are together."

"I heard you; I'm just not understanding you. You and Liam hate each other. Well, you don't hate anyone," He points at me. "But Liam, you've given her nothing but a hard time since she's been back, and Jenna, last time I talked to you, he was a hardheaded asshole."

I wince and glance sideways at Liam apologetically, but he barks out a laugh. "She's not wrong. I was."

"Liam was hurting, and neither of us had any understanding of each other's feelings."

We spend the next twenty minutes going back and forth, telling Mark our story. His face turns from anger to confusion and then finally rests on a sad sort of smile. "Holy shit, you two, this is insane."

"We know." Liam and I say in unison. Then comes the uncontrollable laughter. I can't help myself, and Liam's making it worse. He's laughing so hard he's wheezing. This whole thing is just ridiculous. We are both bent over with our hands on our knees, trying to catch our breath when we look up at Mark. He's looking at us both with the biggest shit-eating grin on his face.

"I haven't heard either of you laugh like that in six fucking years." He claps his hands together loudly. "Yes! I love it! Fuckin' right, you guys!" He steps forward and wraps me in a hug, and Liam comes up beside me and slaps my brother on the back.

I was right. All okay.

CHAPTER

Twelve

Jenna

I signed the lease with Liam this morning. I am officially on my way to entrepreneurship.

He wanted to let me use the space for free, and then he wanted to cut the rent in half. We finally compromised on a discounted rent so that it wouldn't cost him anything to own the shop, and, as long as he was being truthful, he won't make much profit. He didn't want to be earning money at the expense of my new business. On one hand, that's business, but on the other hand, if the roles were reversed, I would feel the exact same. So, I think we worked it out in a way that we can both be happy and successful. There's a fine line between being helpful and undermining my independence, and I need him to stay on the right side of that line. We're still so new; it's only been a few weeks, but Liam knows how important it is to me to be back in Balsam River and doing this for myself. It's what these last six years were for; without this, it would really feel like it was all for nothing.

I am not above accepting help in other ways, though. We've been working away in the shop for the last few weeks. We've been painting and polishing floors. Liam sanded and refinished the old counter that's built into the back wall, and now it's a rich cherry wood colour and gives off such a homey vibe when you come in the door. The large refrigerators that I need to be able to keep the flowers fresh arrived yesterday, and thankfully, Liam, Mark and Noah put their muscles to good use, placing them exactly where I wanted them. Twice. Since I kept changing my mind. Everything's coming together perfectly for my grand opening next Saturday.

I'm mentally running through everything that's done and what still needs to be done by then. I'll need to spend this week preparing arrangements for walk-in purchases and organizing stock and supplies behind the counter for custom orders. The first week of December might seem like an odd time to open a flower shop, but there are so many options for Christmas-themed arrangements that I think it's going to work in my favour. I'm working nonstop on designing wreaths, swags, centrepieces, potted arrangements, as well as floral bouquets. Sherri and Sara are helping me with taking orders and working the cash register on Saturday, but I think after that, I will be good on my own for a bit. I don't know if I will have enough business to warrant a part-time employee once the rush of opening is over. As much as it would be amazing to have so much work that I couldn't handle it myself, the thought of growing so quickly makes me sweat a little. A lot actually.

I just keep telling myself to focus on the now; worry about the future later. As much as I'm trying to stay out of the future, I can't keep my mind from wandering to the past from time to time.

I remember how much Amy always encouraged me to do this. She knew how much flowers meant to me and how they brought me so much joy whenever I was having a hard time as a teen. Every spring, I would walk through the field behind our house until I reached a back paddock of theirs that was completely full of wildflowers. I would pick them and arrange them in a million different ways and then deliver them to Amy, Sara, Mrs. Ryan, my mom, teachers at school, and anyone who I thought might need their day brightened. So, pretty much anyone.

Sometimes, I would fasten them to the front of the horses' stalls, and Mr. Ryan would come in and laugh his big hearty laugh but then bend over and smell them before he took each horse out for its daily exercise. Making people happy made me happy. When my dad left, there wasn't a lot that made sense. I found it hard to be happy in those first few months and noticed my mom was the same, but when I brought her flowers, it cheered us both up. I felt the same way when Amy died. She loved any type of flower so much that I'm sure it'll always be a connection that I feel with her. She always said no one matched the colours like I could. I was never a particularly creative person, but given a field of flowers, that's what I did: I created. I created beauty and that beauty brought joy to people that I loved. I decided one summer when I was in high school that I wanted to do that for the whole town. We'd never had a flower shop in town before, and I was going to be the one to open one.

I can almost feel the warmth of Amy's smile, watching me do what I love, what she always knew I could.

I shake my head a little with a smile and bring my mind back to my to-do list; first, we will see if I can get this all done in time. I have one week, and then it will be the moment of truth.

"The Jenna Special is hot and ready to go!"

"Ah, I love you, Sherri. Have I told you this lately?"

Sherri taps her chin with her pointer finger, "Hmm, not today, I don't think." She grins and laughs as I reach over the counter to give her an awkward hug with the counter between us. She has really been a lifesaver this week. I've never had a best girlfriend, in fact, no one has even come close since Amy and Sara and I were close. But Sherri sure does fill the role. She is wild and energetic and always there when I need her. She's been there to lift heavy boxes and cry over misplaced roses; she listens to me gush over Liam with a smile on her face. She is truly an angel sent to me from Heaven.

"Oh shit, your brother is about to come in the door."

"Oh shit?" I raise one eyebrow at her in question, "That is the opposite of 'oh shit.' You meant to say, 'Oh, yay! Here comes your brother! I'm going to make my move!' I've told you a hundred times that you need to, and there's no time like the present. Besides, I've definitely caught him checking you out, and I can't believe how different he is around you. It's crazy to see, honestly."

She leans in and whispers, "Different, how?"

I love seeing her like this; she almost seems shy and reserved, so *not* Sherri.

"Different, like how you're turning red and whispering to me about him right now, He's usually so loud and obnoxious and doesn't give a crap about what anyone says or thinks. With you, he's quiet and cautious in a way that I've never seen. Dare I say he's smitten with you?" I laugh to myself as she takes that in. Mark is not a bad guy; he's one of the best, actually. He just doesn't have any reservations about saying or doing whatever he wants, when he wants. We've had this conversation before, and I've even tried to suss out Mark to see where he's at, but he shut any inquiries right down, not with denial but with abrupt subject changes, so I'm still certain there's something there.

Mark saunters in with Andi hot on his heels. I squat down to catch her in her running hug that she's famous for, "Hey Andi! How are you home from school so early?"

"Hi, Auntie Jenna! Daddy picked me up today, so I didn't have to take the bus home," she groans and rolls her eyes, "the bus takes forever to get me home."

"I remember that from when I had to ride it, too. You might like it when you're older and can get some homework done before you even get home." She shakes her head vigorously, "Nope, I don't think so. I just want to get home and see Grandpa's cows and horses as fast as I can. I miss them when I'm at school."

"Ha! You sound just like how your mom and Auntie Sara were when they were young. I was lucky enough that they often brought me along, so I got to see the animals, too." She smiles big at the mention of her mom, and it squeezes my heart a little bit. I glance up at Mark to see if it is okay that I mentioned her. I realize that I haven't been around enough to know how everyone handles talking about Amy around Andria, or Mark, for that matter.

Liam and I talk about her so much that it seems so normal to me, and it hurts a lot less than it did. I can smile and laugh at the memories now because there were so many, and she would want us to hold onto those harder than our broken hearts. Mark isn't even paying attention to Andi and me; he's totally engrossed in whatever Sherri is saying. It looks to be a bit more interesting than just his coffee order. I can't help but shake my head and smile.... And they say Liam and I were slow. Okay, maybe these two aren't that bad, but they weren't kidding when they said it was torture to watch us not getting together.

Sherri notices me watching and smiles, passing me a paper bag with a pastry in it for Andi. As I reach for it, Andi squeals, "Is it chocolate, Sherri?"

"It sure is sugar pie!"

"Oh, thank you, thank you!" She chants as she grabs the bag and runs to a table at the front window to rip into her favourite after-school treat, a chocolate Danish.

Mark smiles back at where Andi is sitting and then turns to Sherri, "You're too good to her, you know?"

"She's worth it. That girl's smile could turn a raincloud into a sunbeam." Okay, now I'd say Mark looks like one of those cartoons that have hearts in their eyes that start flying up over their head. Loving Andi is surely the way to his heart, and it looks like Sherri has found her place there. He takes his coffee from her hand and pauses as their fingers touch briefly against the side of the cup.

Do they actually have no clue what is going on here?

He turns and walks over to join Andi at her table, so I take his place at the counter. Leaning over, I whisper, "What. Was. That?"

Her cheeks are bright red now as she says, "He asked me to go to the Winter Festival with him and Andi next Saturday."

"What?" I whisper-yell. "Do you want to scream and jump up and down right now?"

"Maybe!" She beams at me, "Can we go to the back and just get it out of our systems?"

I burst out laughing, "Yes, we definitely can."

Thankfully the week flies by without any major crisis. Sara and Sherri helped me finish up all my half-finished design ideas and were amazing at putting them together, too. I don't know what I would have done without them.

Now here we are. The grand opening is tomorrow, and everyone is here helping pull off this miracle. These girls are everywhere and anywhere and always right here with me. From adding final touches to décor, to making whole new arrangements for the front window. This is all such a dream come true. Not just the flower shop but the people, the love, and the welcome arms this whole town wrapped around me as soon as I came home. The entire shop is decked out in evergreens and holly. Noah and Mark are moving all the finished pots of greenery to the front of the shop so they're ready to be moved outside first thing in the morning. There's a Christmas tree in the front corner of the shop with empty boxes wrapped in Christmas paper underneath it. Our sweet Andi has taken her job of putting the ornaments on the tree very seriously. She's been at it for over an hour. My mom is busy at home making a delicious dinner for us all to relax and eat together when we're done here.

Liam had been helping the guys with all the heavy pots, but I see now he's made his way over to the Christmas tree to help Andi. She's beaming up at him as she passes him another ornament and then points for him to put it in the exact spot she would like. Even standing on a chair, she still has to look up to him and can barely reach to point where she wants it placed. He must get it, though, because he hangs the ornament carefully, and she smiles and claps her hands, "Perfect, Uncle Liam! You did it!"

She looks so much like Amy standing there next to him, the little white Christmas lights reflecting in her eyes. The smile that spreads across his face at her praise melts my heart. He loves her so much, and I can tell by the way he looks at her that he would move mountains for her. Watching them together is making my fingers feel tingly. Again, I need to not think of the future too much and live in the moments that we are given, but I can't help but think of how amazing of a father he will be and how much I want to be the woman to make that happen for him.

As if he can feel my thoughts, he turns to catch me staring. He winks at me with one side of his mouth turned up like he knows what I'm thinking, *because he always knows*. He can read me better than anyone. I think he even has my mom beat. He knows my heart, and by the mega-watt smile he's giving me now, he also knows that it beats for him.

I can't believe I'm standing in the centre of Jenna's Blooms.

It's real, I did it. We did it.

I clap my hands together and spin around, revelling in how amazing this is.

Arms wrap around me from behind. Liam Ryan is wrapping his arms around me. I will never get used to this.

"Are you happy?" His lips brush against my neck just below my ear. Goosebumps rise on my skin, followed by his deep chuckle. He knows the effect he has on me. My smile is so big it's hurting my face. "I don't know if I've ever been this happy."

I turn around in his embrace so that I'm facing him. I wrap my arms around his neck, and my fingers automatically play with the ends of his hair that rest there, just above his shirt collar. Who has goosebumps now? I smile at him knowingly.

"You know exactly what you do to me, don't you, Jenna?"

"You know, Mr. Ryan, I was just thinking the exact same thing about you." He bends slightly and lifts me up and towards him. Instinctively, my legs wrap around his waist, and I can't help but notice that I fit here, in his hands and against his body, so perfectly.

"Were you now?"

"Mmhmm..." He lights my body on fire. His touch, his eyes, that smile. Everything that is Liam is everything that I need. He leans in to kiss me, but I lean back, away from his face, so I can get a better look into his eyes. The mischief in them is almost more than I can take right now. Everyone has left for the day, and I want nothing more than to let myself go and show Liam exactly how much he means to me. I brush his scruffy cheek gently with my fingers. He's smiling now like he knows what I'm thinking. I lean in and kiss his cheek where my fingers just were. Then down his jaw, up to the corner of his mouth and finally to his lips. His hands are under the back of my shirt, seeking anything I will give him. He brings one to my stomach and caresses his way up. It's not enough. I don't think I will ever get enough. The world fades away. Nothing and no one else matters at this moment. It's just us. He makes me believe that maybe this is all we'll ever need, just each other.

CHAPTER

Thirteen

Jenna

T he grand opening of Jenna's Blooms went off without a hitch. It was absolutely amazing. It felt like the whole town came out to support me! We ran completely out of everything I had made ahead of time and took twenty-seven orders for custom arrangements, all varying in size but needed before Christmas! December just got a lot busier, and I couldn't be happier!

It's been a week since then, and I still feel like I'm flying. I wake up every day trying to figure out how I got this lucky, that this is my life now. I head to Liam's for my morning cup of ambition, sometimes from his house, and he drives us into town, and sometimes I meet him there if I stay at mom's overnight. We've made a quick breakfast together a part of our routine and I love it. I feel bad sometimes for the time I'm not spending with my mom, but when we do hang out on the odd evening or on weekends, it's so easy and fun that I know the quality far outweighs quantity. Everything has just fallen so perfectly into place, even for Mom and I.

She seems so happy and relaxed now that Mark and I are both close by. It's like she doesn't need to hover and intrude so much when she can watch over us in close proximity.

After breakfast with Liam, I head down the street to my shop to work away at fulfilling orders and making up bouquets for walk-in customers as I go. I spend my days surrounded by roses, carnations, lilies, and, right now, poinsettias and evergreens. I love it so freaking much. When Sherri is on break from Liam's, she either comes over to chat and work away beside me or if I need to get out of my own head for a bit, I meet her over there for a coffee and snack at our usual table. Sara has started joining us when she can, too. It really feels like Sara, and I have bridged most of the gap that Amy's death and my leaving town caused. I'm sure Liam is helping on that front, but no matter how we've gotten there, I'm so happy to have her as a friend again.

There's nothing like sharing this life with someone who's known you your whole life and takes the good with the bad and loves you through it. I feel like that's what I've finally found.

Sara's been super busy working for The Balsam News; it turns out it isn't just writing that she does there; with the Balsam Winter Festival coming up next weekend, she's been in charge of advertising and marketing the whole thing to the region and beyond. I don't know how she does everything. She's at work more than ten hours a day, and she spends time with Andi several times a week. We all take turns watching her for Mark when he's on his twenty-four-hour shift at the fire station. But Sara seems to take her more than the rest of us, and she's happy to do it; she never complains even a little bit. I think she and Andria have a special bond, being her only maternal aunt. I love Andi more than anything, and I don't think for a second that I'm less of an aunt to her because I'm her father's sister and not her mother's. But there is something to say of the connection between sisters, and then those sisters to their daughters. I think it's like a mother-and-daughter connection being something so unique you can't explain how it's different. It just is. I am definitely not taking offence to it. I don't have a sister, so I can only imagine the loss that Sara felt when Amy died and still feels every day. I can also imagine how much having

Andria back in her life might ease that hurt just a tiny bit. I am so happy for them both to have found some healing and happiness in each other.

I am loving getting to know Andi these past couple of months, too; she is such a little firecracker! More like Mark than Amy in that way. She talks nonstop and asks five hundred questions every time I see her. Liam and I have started taking her out for ice cream after school on Fridays. It's worth it just for the free entertainment. She thinks it's the greatest thing that Uncle Liam and Auntie Jenna are both her aunt and uncle, even though we aren't married yet. She has the whole wedding planned, and her flower girl dress picked out. Every time she brings it up, my cheeks turn pink, but Liam just laughs and squeezes my hand or kisses Andi's forehead and says she'll be the most beautiful flower girl he's ever seen.

Gah! You'll find me on the icy sidewalk in a puddle every time that happens.

He's killing me with how sweet he is and how attentive and loving. He holds doors and brings me coffee. He walks me to my car, even when it's only ten feet from the door. He kisses my forehead and plays with my hair. He is so perfect that I feel like sometimes I'm waiting for the other shoe to fall. He says there is no other shoe. He's wearing them both.

Ha-ha, he's so funny. I've perfected my eye roll these last weeks with him and his cheesy comebacks. But honestly, I think I've just missed this for so many years that I forgot what it could be like to be loved and to love someone with everything that I am.

We spend most of our evenings snuggled in front of his TV, sometimes watching movies we loved as kids, sometimes watching new ones for the first time, sometimes not watching TV at all.

Tonight, we're watching Friends reruns because… well, for no reason, really, it's the best TV show ever made, and we both love it. We've seen every episode at least ten times, so it's sort of just on in the background; I wonder if now would be a good time to bring up my house hunting. I want to talk to him about it, but I don't know if it's something he would want to be a part of or if he even cares. I know he cares about me, obviously, but he's not going to live in this house. It's just something that I want to do for me, to say that I've bought my home and been a successful entrepreneur. I know I won't end up there, so he might think it's pointless, but I really want his input and knowledge to help me with the decision.

I turn to him on the couch and say, "I want to start looking for a house in the next couple of months. Will you come with me to look at some around town?"

His frown surprises me, as do the words that come out of his mouth, "No, I won't. Why are you going to look at houses?"

I want to explain, but now I feel like I need to be cautious. I'm not sure where the angry tone he's using is coming from, "Well," I draw out the word to give him time to process where this conversation might be going, "if the shop keeps up being this busy, I haven't had to use much of my savings because Mom won't take any money for me living with her, so I can move out sooner than I thought. The shop started turning a profit so much faster than I ever dreamed, so as much as I don't want to get too far ahead of myself, I really want to get out of my childhood bedroom with its single bed."

He stands up from the couch abruptly and starts pacing back and forth in front of the TV. "So, you're just going to buy a house? In town?" He says that last part incredulously, like it hasn't been my plan all along.

"Liam, what is going on? Why are you being this way? You knew this was what I had always planned. Of course, I want to buy a house, and yes, in town. Do you think I can afford to buy ten acres down the road from you? Are you insane right now?" I can tell he's not even listening to me, so I raise my voice, "Will you please stop pacing?"

He looks at me. His hair is standing on end now from him pushing his fingers through it in frustration. He glares at me and says, "Am I insane? No Jenna, I am not insane. I'm wondering where you're even coming from. If after everything we've been through and these last two months that we've spent together, you still just want to buy a house and carry on with your life plan like I don't even exist." He sits down in the chair on the opposite side of the living room now, as far away from me as he can get without leaving the room.

Shit, I read this whole thing wrong. Is he suggesting I move in here?

"Are you suggesting I move in here?"

He lifts his face from where he had it resting in his hands, "No .... Yes. I don't know! God, Jenna, I just didn't think you were going to make any major moves right now. You buying a house feels like a giant step away from me."

I go to him and kneel on the floor in front of him. I take his hands in mine and kiss both of his palms like he did to me once when I needed reassurance. "Liam, you are the love of my life. I will never take any steps away from you ever again. We never talked about moving in together. It's only been a couple of months, and I need to get out of my mother's house, so I just assumed that I would buy my own place like I always planned, and I'm sorry that I didn't consider how that would make you feel. I honestly didn't think it would change anything between us. We spend so many nights together here, and we'll keep doing that, but maybe we could spend some at my place too. I think it's important for us to have our own spaces right now, though."

"Why? I don't need space from you. I want you here all the time. The only reason I said no that I wasn't suggesting you move in is because, like you said, it has only been a couple of months. But time doesn't matter to me, Jenna. I've loved you for a decade, and that's not going to change in the next six months or years."

"I don't know if it's so much that I need space from you, Liam, because I don't. I agree with you that time shouldn't matter, and I know without a doubt that my feelings for you are not going to change, but I think I just need a space to call mine. This house is yours; my mom's house is hers; my apartment was owned by some multi-millionaire in Toronto. I want my own home, even if it's just for a little while."

"I guess that answers my next question. If you would consider renting in town and moving in here sooner rather than later?"

"I don't think so, babe. I really want this for me. I set goals, and I need to reach them. I make plans, and I have to follow through. Not for no reason but because they're important to me, and they make me feel like I have some control over my life. We know better than most how much is truly out of our control. I just need this. I need it for me." He looks into my eyes and looks so sad. I don't know how to make this better for him and stay true to myself.

"What is our plan then, Jenna? What are your goals for us?"

That catches me off guard. I don't know why; I should have thought about these things, but I've just been so happy and focusing on the present that I may have done that a little too well. I didn't let myself think past today, not in too much detail anyway.

"I don't know, I haven't really thought about it."

He winces at my words and pulls his hands out of mine, "Liam, I'm sorry, that's not what I mean. I just mean that I'm so happy with you that I've just been living each day in the moment."

"Well, that's great for you, Jenna; I'm glad you've been so 'present.' While you've been enjoying that, I've been planning our future. I've been dreaming of you in my bed every night, not just when it's too late for you to go home. I've been picturing you walking down an aisle toward me in a white lace gown, holding a bouquet of white roses; I've been seeing you with your belly swollen with my baby and you sleeping on that couch–" he points behind me at the couch we were just snuggled on ten minutes ago, was that just ten minutes ago? His voice cracks with emotion, "On that couch, with our baby asleep on your chest. I don't know what I was planning and thinking all of this for if you're just moving into a house on your own that you insist on wasting your money on owning. What was it all for Jenna? Are any of those dreams even on your radar? Do you even want a future with me?"

Fuck, now I'm crying because I want all those things, and he's so hurt and so angry. It's not that we want different things, but is it just that we want them at different times? I don't even know what we're fighting about anymore.

"Of course, I want a future with you! I want all of that. I don't even know what we're fighting about. I want what you want. All of it. With you. It'll only ever be you. I just need a bit of time to make a space that is mine. Maybe it's just to know that I can. I don't even really know why. But I know that I want to live here with you too. I love this house, it's perfect. It's yours now, but it will be ours one day. I just want my own first, just for a time. Can you wait for me just a little bit longer? I promise I'll be right here; I'm not going anywhere."

CHAPTER

Fourteen

Liam

My head is spinning, and it's too fucking hot in here. Why is it so hot? I want her to leave, and I want to pull her into my arms and never let her out of my house at the same time. What is happening to me?

How can I make her see that she doesn't need this bullshit time she's talking about? She needs to be here with me, in this house; it will be hers as much as mine. I just don't understand where she's coming from, and it's breaking my heart to think she doesn't want me the same way I want her.

She's saying all the right things but then says she's buying her own house anyway. It just doesn't make sense.

Her soft voice breaks into my thoughts, "Liam, say something. What can I do? Tell me how to fix this baby. I love you.

"Stay. Move in with me. The future starts now. I want you here beside me for the rest of my life. If it's too soon to get married, then please at least move in."

"Ugh, Liam! You're not hearing me. Every tomorrow that we spend together is our future. I love you, and I will move in here, and I will marry you, but not right now. I can't."

How does she have the nerve to be yelling at me right now? I'm the one who's hurt and pissed off. Where does she get off?

"Then just go, Jenna. Go home, go house shopping, go be whoever it is you think you need to be, proving fuck all to no one because no one gives a shit if you did any of this on your own! We aren't meant to be alone, Jen! We're meant to be together, but whatever, fuck right off and do your own thing if that's what you want."

She's crying now, fucking great. I get up to leave the room. I can't look at her if she's crying, but I can't help her either. She did this. This time, it's on her.

Somewhere in the back of my mind, I realize that I thought that last time, for six years I blamed her for my own assumptions. But this time is different. She should be here with me. If we're committed to each other, then what I'm asking isn't too much.

"Liam." Her voice is soft and broken in sobs now.

"Jenna, please, go."

"I love you, Liam, don't do this."

I can't take another minute of this. I walk down the hall, into my bedroom and close the door.

I didn't sleep for more than fifteen minutes last night, and Jenna hasn't been in for her coffee yet this morning. That's enough to make me want to rip the door off its hinges and go find her. Sherri's been giving me the side eye all morning, too, like she knows something is up.

Shit, knowing those girls, she probably knows more than I do. I still don't know how that went so sideways. I thought we were on the same page this whole time. I'm trying not to ask her if she knows where Jenna is and how she's doing this morning when she steps out from behind the counter with two paper coffee cups in hand, one of which I can guarantee is Jenna's, she changed her morning order from her vanilla dark roast after I got her to try Sherri's famous maple latte. She's not coming.

A half-hour later, Sherri's still not back, but Mark and Noah push into my office. "Hey, dipshit, you already fucked up?"

Ugh, why, God, why did you bless me with these assholes for brothers. Noah, I can blame God, Mark, I can't even blame Amy. I chose him long before she did.

I throw my hands up in defence, "Hold on! Why do you think I'm the one who fucked up?"

They both burst out laughing.

Like I said, assholes.

Mark starts, "Listen, Jenna told us what went down. She wanted to know from our perspective if she was out of line."

"Aaand?" I draw the word out, hoping they get the hint to the answer I want them to give me.

"And...we think you fucked up already."

"What? Why? How?"

"Hold on, hold on," they both have their hands up now.

"Guys, we're just sitting enjoying a nice night together—"

"Ah! Okay, okay, gross. Too much info, too much info, she's our sister!"

I can't help the smile that comes to my face. These two, if nothing else, are hilarious, "Noah, she's not your sister, and I wasn't being gross; for real, we were just watching TV, and she dropped this bomb on me about buying a house by herself! What else was I supposed to do with that but lose my shit? That she doesn't have any intention of moving in with me or starting our future together."

Noah squints his eyes at me in glare, "She's going to be my sister-in-law one day, and I love her like one now, so when I see her crying over a bouquet of roses from something my dumbass brother did, I'm gonna kick his ass, no matter what he thinks is right or wrong."

"She was crying? Today?"

Mark's turn to give me the eye, "Yeah man, she thinks it's over between you two. We know that's bullshit, but what the fuck is wrong with you that you're letting her sit over there thinking that?"

"Listen, Mark, I know she's your sister, so you won't want to hear my side, but she fuckin' blindsided me!"

"She told us. She said she caught you off guard, and she tried to apologize and explain her feelings, and you shut her out."

Did I do that? Did I shut her out when she was trying to open up? I don't think I did, but...

"What did she say?"

"She said she wants to be with you while following through with the plans she's always had for herself and her independence in this town. She wants to meet her needs before yours so that when you two start your life together, she can put you and have a family with you first. With no regrets or reservations. Made perfect sense to me, brother. I don't see the problem."

"Fuck me." I'm mumbling to myself under my breath, but Mark hears me and has to get in a "No thanks, Liam, I don't swing that way," Always lightening the mood with a laugh. I can't stop the breath of a laugh. It's hard to laugh for real when my chest feels like it's caving in. They make it sound so simple, but how can I get them to see how much that plan may be perfect for her? It hurts me. "Guys, you're making me feel like an asshole---"

Noah claps his hands and turns to leave, "Perfect, my job here is done."

Mark bursts out laughing, and I can't help but shake my head and laugh with them.

"Listen. I can't make you see my side, and I can't change how all that shit made me feel. It made me feel insignificant. Like she has bigger plans than just being with me."

"When we came in here, you said she had no plans of being with you, and that's just not true, Liam. You're blinded by your fear of losing her again. You're hearing shit she's not saying." I rub my hands up and down over my face, "Maybe. Okay…maybe that's true. But I also think it's valid that I want to be a part of the plans that my girlfriend is making for her life. It is supposed to be our life, not just hers. She's acting like I'm an afterthought. Do you guys have any idea what that feels like?"

They look at each other and laugh again, "Nope, our beds are empty at night," Mark interrupts Noah, "Well, mine is anyway. We know Noah's is in the morning, at least, so that's something."

Noah throws his head back, laughing, but doesn't deny it, "So maybe we aren't the right guys for this conversation in the first place."

Mark stops him and says, "In all seriousness, Liam, I do get how you're feeling. I remember what it was like to be a team with Amy. I remember knowing she had my back, and our plans were made together, not separately. I know you and Jenna aren't married, but you're clearly on your way to that, so maybe she did go about all of this big future stuff the wrong way. I get it, I do, but you need to talk to her about this. You can't keep flying off the handle and walking away instead of talking and dealing with your shit. She's a reasonable person, and she loves you; the problem is, I can guarantee you, she isn't going to change her plans. Can you live with that? Because what she was trying to explain to you isn't going anywhere. She needs to do this part of her life for herself. Can you respect that?"

"I want to. I love her so much it hurts Mark. I just don't get what the difference is to her; if she knows she's going to move in with me later, why not now? If she knows that she wants a life with me, then why wait? We know how fucking fragile life is, and I don't want to waste one day of however many I have with her."

Noah jumps in, always philosophical Noah, "If you know she's all in and is going to make all those commitments, albeit, down the road, then why can't you wait? We can go back and forth all day, but eventually, someone has to cave. There really is no difference in both of your desired outcomes. Unless one of you dies before the future gets here." I groan at his crudeness, but he nailed it. That is the problem: we never know how much time we have. He ignores my groan and carries on, "And I know that's what you're afraid of, that's what we're all afraid of. But when that fear starts pushing the people we love away, rather than having us living life to the fullest, then we've messed something up. She is yours. She is all in; she will fulfill all her dreams with you. Not in spite of you, not before you, or after, but with you, if you let her."

Mark starts a slow clap, and Noah bows, these assholes, seriously.

"Okay, I get it. I'll go find her. Is she still working?" I look at my watch and can't believe it's noon already. Maybe I can take her lunch, and we can talk this out again.

Mark looks at his watch and must have the same idea because he stands up, "Shit, I gotta get home and get stuff done before I have to get Andi from school. Liam, please remember that you can't fight with her to try to change her plans. She needs your forgiveness for the way she made them, but she's not going to give them up. Her part is that she's going to have to forgive you for walking out on her when you didn't like the way things were going. You both need to grow the fuck up, honestly."

He laughs and slaps me on the back, and I pull him in for a hug. We don't do 'bro hugs or handshakes' anymore. Another thing grief changed for us, but I like this better anyway.

"Thanks, Mark. I appreciate you giving me the benefit of the doubt and taking the time to talk to me," I point my finger at my brother, "This idiot has no choice but to listen to me, but you didn't have to, so thank you, it means a lot."

He steps back and smiles, "Forget about worrying about these days being spent apart instead of living together and start cherishing the days no matter where she lives. Just love her while you have her, okay?" My heart clenches when I think of what it would be like to lose Jenna; I nod my head, "You're right, I will."

We all head out into the coffee shop to leave, but Mark stops abruptly when he sees Sherri's smiling face behind the counter. I slap him on the back as I walk by him, chuckling, "Same advice to you, bud, cherish that one too. She's one of the good ones." His face flushes just a little, but enough I can tell as he says, "Yeah, no kidding."

He walks over to the counter and leans over it reaching to place his hands on either side of her face and plants a kiss right on her lips. Noah and I burst out laughing while Sherri's hands wrap around his neck, keeping him from retreating to his side of the counter.

"Okay, okay, this is my place of business! That's enough! Happy for you and all, but let's take it to the back next time the urge to make out with my barista strikes you."

Noah is howling now, and some patrons join in while others start clapping and.... Okay, they aren't stopping. Alright, I'm outta here. I have my own girl to woo today.

Jenna is behind the counter fussing over a flower arrangement that already looks perfect to me, but she'll change minute details until it's exactly what she has pictured in her mind.

I'm standing on the street watching her through the window; she hasn't noticed me yet, so I can see her without her guard up. The guys weren't kidding, I fucked up, at least she's not crying now, but she looks so morose I almost can't stand to look at her, knowing I caused her pain. Before I look like a creeper standing out here peering in the window, I move to go in the door.

She lifts her head at the bell chiming over the door; her face instantly changes from pained to blank. That's not a good sign. I start with a simple "Hi."

"Hi." She bends her head back to the flowers she's working on; I notice she's just putting them back where they just were, avoiding me for roses. Fair. I deserve that.

"Can we talk?"

"Liam, I don't know. I tried talking to you, and if I remember correctly, you walked away and locked yourself in your room like a 12-year-old, so

I'm not really sure if there's any point."

"Jenna, come on, I'm sorry if I overreacted, but you really caught me off guard with all your plans."

"Why? They weren't new plans. That's what I don't understand, why was any of that surprising to you?"

I step up the counter; it's the only way I can get closer to her, "Because I thought they'd changed. Okay? I'm sorry, but I can't help what I feel and what I thought you felt. We've gone over this, Jenna. I didn't come here to fight. I came here to talk to you and to apologize."

She puts the flowers down, finally, and looks up at me, surprised, "You want to apologize?"

"Yes, I'm sorry for overreacting and for trying to press my plans and ideas on you at the expense of your own. I mean it when I say that I can't help how I feel. I want all the things I told you last night, and I wish you wanted them on the same timeline that I did, but with some help from our brothers, I realize that you do want them, and I just have to be patient. I disregarded your dreams and ambitions, and I didn't mean to, and I promise I will do my best not to do that again. I just don't want to waste one second that we have together, but I see now that none of that time matters if you're not happy and fulfilled. I don't want to take anything from your life, Jenna. I only want to add to it."

She has tears in her eyes, but she's not smiling, her beautiful smile that I thought that speech would bring out. Why does nothing go as I expect it to?

"Jenna, say something."

"Thank you."

"Thank you? That's it."

"Yes, I'm sorry if you were expecting more, but I don't know if I have more to give right now. I didn't expect my plans to affect you in such a severe way, and I don't know if I'm ready for that level of reliance on each other in this relationship. You were shattered last night when you thought I didn't love you enough to make plans for our future the same as you have. I was shattered this morning when I thought you didn't love me enough to put my needs and dreams ahead of your own and to talk about them with me. I don't know if we deserve to be shattered any more than we already have been in this lifetime, Liam. I don't want to ever be the one to bring you heartache. I can't be that person. I just need some time to think before we put ourselves back in that position."

No... no way. Time to think? She can't be serious. This can't be happening. She doesn't want to bring me heartache, but she stands there telling me that she doesn't know if she's ready for this and she needs time to think.

I run my hands through my hair, trying to calm my fraying nerves. I want to scream, not at her, just at this situation. How did everything get so fucked up so quickly? "Jenna, babe, you don't mean that. Don't make this bigger than it is. We can work through all of this together."

"Liam, I hope we can. I'm not saying we're over; we mean more to me than that. I'm just saying I don't know what's next right now."

"No, what's next is living each day that we're given the best we can, together, like you said, some nights at my house and others at yours, until you're ready to move in with me, or we can buy another house together. Whatever you want. That's what's next, Jenna, you and me, us, together."

"I just need time, Liam, I'm sorry."

"Tell me what I can do. I'm not living this miscommunication trope again. We are going to talk about everything all the way through this. I will leave here today, but I will see you tomorrow. You will come in for your coffee in the morning, no more of this Sherri delivering bullshit, and we will have breakfast. You can tell me about your days, and we will check in, see how you're feeling about the future, and we can go house hunting. We'll find you the perfect one. Okay? We're going to do all those things; you're not walking away from us?"

Her lips lift into a small smile, a sad one, but it's a smile, "Okay, Liam, we can do those things. We will see how it goes. Can I ask, though, what do you know about miscommunication tropes?"

I give her my signature crooked smile that I know she loves, "I do own a bookstore, you know? I know how all the romance novels go, and I will not be living in one anymore." That gets a laugh out of her. A little less sad than the smile, a lot less sad than when I got here. I have to take the wins and go with it. I walk behind the counter to give her a kiss. She hesitates but doesn't stop me. That's something at least. "I'll see you tomorrow. I love you."

"I love you too, Liam."

CHAPTER

Fifteen

Jenna

This week has been hell. My fight with Liam last Sunday has taken its toll on me. I'm not sleeping, and I barely have any appetite. It didn't seem to help at all that he came on Monday and apologized. I thought that was all I needed until I got it, and I was still feeling so scared and unsure. We have seen each other every day, just like he said, but nothing is the same. I'm not the same; he's grovelling, and I don't love it. He apologized, and that should be enough, but he's living in fear now, fear of losing me. Theoretically, that sounds very sweet, but it's not what I want for him. I know what it feels like because the way he turned so quickly last weekend and walked away from me, literally and emotionally, brought out the same fears in me. I don't want to live on the edge of worrying about upsetting him or that he's just going to bail when things don't go his way.

I've talked extensively about this with Mark and Sherri. I'm treading lightly with Sara since he is her brother, after all. Even Mark and Sherri think it's time that I put my pride aside and just let us live. I just feel like this arm's length I've been keeping him at this week will give me time to figure out how I really feel about all his future plans. Although I can admit, never out loud, of course, I have noticed that it's not really working.

I thought everything he wanted was what I wanted, but never if it meant losing myself, too. I can't wrap my head around how volatile his reaction was. I don't want to put him in that situation again, for his sake and my own. But God, I miss him. I miss his arms around me when I wake up in the middle of the night, I miss the closeness that we've had these past few months, and I miss finishing each other's sentences and cooking dinner together. I miss us.

Today isn't a day that I'll have time to dwell on that.

It's the Balsam Winter Festival, and the shop has been flooded with customers as the town is teaming up with out-of-towners here for the festival. Despite the opportunity to make extra profits, there's a town-wide agreement that everyone will close early to enjoy the festival at its fullest. There are street vendors selling crafts and homemade wares. There are always lots of vendors selling baked goods and, of course, hot chocolate and hot cider. Food trucks line Maple Ave to provide anything you could possibly want for supper. The most exciting part of the festival this year is that Mark and Sherri are on their first real date today. With Andi and the rest of us in tow of course, but I told them Andi could have a sleepover with me tonight so that they can have their evening just the two of them. Mom is away at some gardening conference down south, so I have the house to myself, and if I'm honest, I'm lonely. A girl's night with my favourite niece is exactly what I need! I think hanging out with Liam in the group today will be a nice change of pace. Maybe it will lighten some of our conversations. We've talked about everything until we're just talking in circles, but I think it will be great to get outside and just have some fun with him today.

They're all meeting over at Liam's to pick up coffees and then picking me up here on their way by. Just as I'm locking the till, I see Andi's little face peek through the window. A quick glance shows me Mark and Sherri aren't far behind her down the sidewalk. I rush out the door and swing her up into my arms. "Hello, my little darling!" I coo at her. She responds with an exaggerated British accent, "Hello, my little Auntie!" We both dissolve into giggles because that's how we've been greeting each other this week, for some reason, and everyone thinks we're crazy. We most definitely are and I love it.

Mark and Sherri lean in for hugs as they shake their heads at our crazy antics. Sara comes up behind me with a tray of coffee cups, and I reach around them to give her a hug, "Hey, coffee for me?" I ask, pointing at the tray hopefully. She laughs, "Of course, one maple latte for you," she says as she passes me a cup. "Noah! Get over here and take yours then I can carry mine and toss this tray."

Noah rushes up from where he's looking in a shop window further down the street, "Christmas shopping, Noah?"

"Maybe! What's it to you, Jenna? Mind your own business!" He whines like a child as he shoves my shoulder gently. I laugh and revel in the warmth spreading through my chest. My heart is so full this year, the best thing I ever could have done was move back here. These people are my people, and I love them all so much. Speaking of people I love, Liam isn't here. That's weird.

"Hey, where's Liam? Lagging behind again as usual?" I ask no one in particular.

Apparently, I need to ask someone in particular because no one answers me. I look to Noah and then to Mark, "Hello? Where's Liam?"

They both look back and forth from each other and back to me and finally, Mark says, "Uh... he's... uh..."

"Mark. What's wrong? You're scaring me! Where is he?"

Noah cuts in, "He's not coming."

"What? Not coming? Why?" Mark rests his hand on my forearm before he says, "He's just having such a hard time, sis. He's really struggling. I think he just needed to be alone tonight."

"Struggling? With what?"

"Come on, Jenna, you can't be that stupid."

"Okay, okay. I know things haven't been that great between us, but he's been fine, better than fine, actually. He's always bringing me coffee and helping me in the shop, and all smiles, so I don't know what you're talking about when you say he can't be here tonight because he's struggling."

"I think that all might have been an act so that he didn't break in front of you. Being with you, without being with you? It's killing him, Jenny, you gotta do something. Either apologize or cut him loose. I don't know, this is awful for us, and we're just spectators."

Noah is standing beside me now, and Sara comes up on the other side. I look to each of them for confirmation that what Mark is saying is true. The sad look in their eyes is all the confirmation I need.

"Wait, apologize? What do I need to apologize for?" Mark lets out an exasperated sigh, and Sherri grabs his hand. She calms him. I love that, but I don't love that he needs to be calmed to tell me whatever he's about to tell me.

"Oh, come on! For blindsiding him with your 'independent woman' bullshit, you know he had no idea you hadn't changed your mind about all that. You jump into a serious relationship with your best friend and don't change a single thing that you had planned before you moved back and then freak out because he freaked out. Way to be a team player, Jen. That's not how relationships work. You two are fu—dging," he glances down at Andi, who's engrossed in the earrings the lady at the closest table is selling, then he whispers, "You two are fucking annoying. Get your shit together, apologize and move on with both of your plans."

I'm a little stunned at Mark's outburst, but no one else seems to be. Sherri, Sara, and Noah are all nodding, with the addition of a smirk on Noah's face. He seems to get much amusement out of everyone's relationship woes. I don't really have a comeback for that, much to my chagrin. It's not every day my brother one-ups me with his insults. I'll let him have it today because I think he might be right. I need to think this through once and for all and get my shit together. I don't have much to think through because I know I can't live another day without Liam in my arms.

CHAPTER

Sixteen

Liam

My phone vibrating off the bedside table wakes me up from my restless sleep. Who the fuck is calling me at 1 a.m.?

If Noah is drunk at some bar, I'm going to kill him for waking me for that bullshit. I pick up my phone and squint from the light that the screen gives off. Shit, its Jenna. God, please let her be okay. I swipe to answer, "Jenna? What's going on? Are you okay?"

My chest tightens as I hear that she's breathing heavily, and it sounds like she's been crying, but I think it might beat right out of my chest when she says, "I'm okay, but I need you, Liam; it's Andria."

I don't even remember getting dressed and getting in my car, but I'm at Jenna's door. I don't bother knocking; I just run in with no clue where they are, but I'm driven by a burning need to get to them.

"Jenna!" I yell as soon as the door is closed behind me.

She comes down the stairs in front of me. She's not rushing, so her panic has receded, that's a good sign. Her hair is half out of her ponytail, strewn every which way and her pyjama shorts are on backwards. I can't even take a moment to enjoy the rumpled 'just woke up' look because her face is tear-streaked, and her hands are shaking.

She falls into my arms off the bottom step. I stroke the back of her hair gently as she starts sobbing. "Ssshhh, Jenna, it's okay. I'm here now, baby, where's Andi? How is she doing?"

She hiccups through her sobs and says, "She's asleep now, but she's still so hot, Liam, I don't know what to do."

I lift her under her knees and wrap my other arm around her back. She instinctively wraps her arms around my neck and rests her head on my chest. Despite Andi being sick and Jenna being so distraught, nothing has ever felt so right. This is where she belongs, even if she doesn't realize it yet.

I carry her up the stairs with ease and turn left into what I remember is Mark's childhood bedroom. Andi is sleeping peacefully in his tiny bed. She looks flushed, and her bangs are damp with sweat; there's a damp cloth on the bed table, too, though, so maybe it's from that. Here's hoping anyway. I set Jenna down on the bed beside her, "Just rest here with her, Jen. When was the last time she threw up?"

"I don't know. I think about ten minutes before I called you. Her temp is 102.4, though! I don't know what to do to get it down. We don't have any medicine for kids, Liam. I don't know what I'm doing. Should we take her to the hospital?"

I hold her cheek in my hand, "Sshh, calm down, you're fine, she's fine, you're doing everything right. Did she have any water before she fell asleep?"

"No, she wouldn't, and then she fell asleep, so I thought that was a good thing."

"It is, it is. She needs fluids, but we can wake her in a bit to try. Is the cloth for her forehead?" She sits up and presses her palms into her eyes, "Yes, but it didn't help. Nothing helped. I think she needs a doctor."

I place the cloth back on Andi's little head and sit down to rub Jenna's back, "Not yet, this is fine. 102 is high, but it is not dangerous. Her body is fighting whatever it is that's making her sick. We can check her temp again in 15 minutes and wake her up to see if she can keep some water down. The damp cloth on her head and having her tucked into bed is the best thing for her. She needs rest, but so do you, Jenna. You look wiped." I move to kneel on the floor in front of where she's sitting and take her hands in mine. Thankfully, they've stopped shaking.

She leans forward so that her forehead is resting against mine, "Liam, I was so scared. She couldn't stop throwing up, and then her temp went up so fast, and Mark must have his phone on silent. He didn't pick up, and I didn't know who else to call. I'm sorry for waking you and making you come over here in the middle of the night."

"Don't ever apologize for calling me. I am yours to call. Always."

"But you didn't come to the festival. I know you didn't want to be near me, and then I threw myself into your life in the middle of the night."

"Jenna, I always want to be near you, I was trying to be respectful of what you need, but the second that you need me, I will be here every damn time."

"I'm so sorry for everything this week, Liam; it was awful of me to make such huge plans without you. I was afraid to include you, I think; I was afraid of you not wanting to be a part of them, and at the same time afraid of what it meant to make plans this huge with you. Thank you for understanding and being so amazing this week. Thank you for being here now. God, I don't know what I'd do without you."

We stand up together, still holding hands, so I can wrap her in a proper hug. "It's okay; we can talk about all that later." Then she pulls her head back to look me in the eye. "How do you know so much about sick kids anyway?"

I bark out a laugh, "Ha! I don't, you did everything already, and I googled on my way over here." She smacks my chest playfully and looks over at Andi sleeping, "I guess we should check her temp again and maybe try Mark again---" As she finishes that sentence, her phone starts ringing. It's Mark. I grab the thermometer to check Andi while she answers.

Jenna explains everything that happened to him. Her temp has come down to 100 degrees now, so he's not worried, but he offers to come get her if Jenna wants. We opt to wake her to say goodnight to her dad and sip some water before she passes the phone back to her auntie and falls right to sleep.

I guide Jenna's half-asleep form back to her childhood bedroom and ease her down onto her tiny bed, the house of tiny beds, I guess this is why she wants her own place.

I sit beside her since I don't think I could fit any other way. It's okay for tonight. I'll crash on the couch downstairs. I brush her hair out of her face and gently ease her hair elastic out of her hair. I lean down and kiss her gently on her forehead and whisper, "Goodnight, my love."

She smiles, even though I'm pretty sure she's already asleep.

I peek back into Andi's room on my way downstairs, and she looks just as peaceful as Jenna did. I have an exhausted woman, a sick little girl, and somehow my heart has never been fuller. Because, at the end of the day, when she's tired, stressed and needs help, it's me she calls, and it's me that will always be here for her.

We're going to be okay.

CHAPTER

Seventeen

Liam

Christmas in Balsam River is the busiest time of year for anyone who lives here. All the small-town shops and Jack's Christmas tree farm tend to attract more tourists than any other time of year. For those of us who own those businesses, it's certifiably insane.

Jenna and I are good now, better than good actually, but I feel like I barely see her. We have been through a few houses that she thought she loved but as soon as we stepped foot inside them, she said they weren't the one for her. I keep biting my tongue because all I can think of is how this is a formality, like a rite of passage for her, but she doesn't plan on staying in whatever house she chooses anyway! I can't get past how silly this all feels to me, but I will respect her wishes, hence the tongue-biting. Her happiness is more important than my logic.

With just over one week until Christmas, we are going to be busier than we've been, but I am determined to make this the best Christmas Jenna has ever had.

Christmases have tended to be on the quieter side at our farm since Amy passed away. Nothing has ever been the same throughout the year, but Christmas still hits especially hard. Last year was better with Mark and Andria being back. Mom and Dad really embraced finally having their only grandchild under their roof for Christmas dinner. It was the first time I'd really seen my mom's eyes light up since losing Amy. That little girl is like a balm for the heart.

Now, with Jenna back home, too, I'm hoping we can all gather at the farm together, with her mother, too, of course, and celebrate the season that is supposed to be full of joy and loved ones.

I'm meeting Jenna today to look at one more house before Christmas; Jamie is closing his real estate office tomorrow until the new year but made time to show her this house because he thinks it's perfect for her. We'll see. If she ever gets here. I'm looking at my watch to see just how late she is when she pulls up to the curb behind me. She hops out of her car and runs to my door before I even have a chance to open it. Yes, when I say runs, I mean she runs. Her beaming smile makes every minute that she's late worth the wait. Every argument over mundane things and every crazy idea she has is worth that smile she's giving me right now.

God, I love this girl.

She's bouncing on her toes and rubbing her hands together. "Isn't it so cute! Look at the porch; it's so perfect. I love it already. Don't you?"

"Hello to you too. How was your day?" I deadpan, trying to be annoyed with her for being late but failing miserably. As I step out of my truck, she throws herself into my arms. "Oh, shush you! Jamie's not even here yet, and I'm just excited, okay? I think this is the one!"

"Speak of the devil," I say as Jamie pulls into the driveway of the house; we walk to meet him at the front door. Jenna's not wrong; this porch is great, about ten feet for the depth and runs from end to end of the whole front of the house with a nice high roof over it. She will love sitting out here reading during summer storms. As we step in through the front door, I notice how thick the door frame is; the house is old, made back when they did it right. It's got good bones; I can tell that already. Jenna squeals in excitement from the kitchen; I follow the sound and see her spinning in the large open-concept room; there's no island, and the dining table is also over in an open-concept adjoining room, so the kitchen is a completely wide-open space for her to do her spinning. This girl... I can't help but laugh. I can see her here, baking with Andi and having the dance parties they like to have.

"Oh babe, it's perfect, isn't it?" She coos. I couldn't fake how happy I am for her if I wanted to; I smile back at her, "Ya, hun, it is. It's totally you. I can see you making this place your own."

She gets a running start and jumps to climb me like a koala, swinging her legs around my waist. My hands reflexively go to her ass and support her. I laugh and spin her around like she was doing before I came in. I think my favourite thing about Jenna is that she doesn't have any inhibitions about showing her excitement and passion about something. She's usually quite reserved, but when something gets her excited, she transforms into another person. This happy, carefree 'smiling so big her face must be hurting' person that is in my arms right now is my favourite version of her. If supporting her in her goals and dreams is all it takes to bring this out in her, I can do it in my sleep.

"Okay, you two, it's not your place yet. Take it somewhere more private, eh?"

"Ha-ha, Jamie, you're so funny." Jenna slides down my chest until her feet hit the floor. "I'm just so excited! You were totally right; it's perfect! I want to put an offer in."

Jamie claps his hands together and says, "That's great, Jenna. There haven't been a lot of bites on this one. People just don't respect the character an old home has anymore. I'll put it in before I leave for the holidays, but we won't be able to move forward with much until the new year; is that okay with you?"

"Of course! That's perfect; thank you so much for everything. I know I've been a bit of a pain in your ass, but I'm so happy we persevered and found this gem."

Jamie laughs and gives my girl a hug. He's a good guy. He knows when it's worth it to be patient. He pulls away from her and says, "You know Jenna, this place is special. I know you don't plan on staying here too long, but it would make an amazing rental property, too. You should think about renting it out after you two tie the knot."

Jenna looks to me and then back to Jamie. "That's a great idea, definitely something to think about. Liam and I will talk about it, and maybe you can help us with that when the time comes."

My heart stutters to hear her consider me when making this decision. I know we talked about doing that from now on, and she apologized for the way she went about all this house stuff, but this is the first time we've had the chance to see how we're going to do this stuff together.

I am a cheesy asshole. Look what this girl has done to me.

And I couldn't be happier.

Jenna

"You found a house?" Sherri and Sara both scream at the same time.

"Yes! And it's so cute and so perfect."

"Oh, Jen, I'm so happy for you! What does Liam think? Is he still okay?" Sara is always first to worry about Liam, and I love that for him. He needs someone watching his back since he's always looking out for everyone else.

"Yes! He is better than okay. I think he's genuinely as happy as I am, maybe because the house is such a great fit! Jamie suggested that I hang onto it as an income property after I move in with Liam, so we talked about that for a long-time last night, and we both think that's an amazing idea. It makes the whole thing feel like less of me being a stubborn brat and more about a business opportunity." I laugh because I know these ladies get my independent streak, but it took Liam and Mark a hot minute to understand where I was coming from. Noah seemed to get it right away, but he's always been a little more in tune with different mindsets, not as hard-headed as the rest of them.

Sherri claps her hands. "Well, let's celebrate!"

"I don't have the house yet! I just put an offer in. Hopefully, it will all go through in the new year, and I'll be able to move into my own home in a matter of weeks."

"Oh well, it's as good as done. We can still have a girl's night and toast your new home and business venture!" We all agree and stand up from the table at Liam's that we've been occupying for the last half hour.

I smile big and clap my hands together. "What time are you off, Sherri? I can meet you anytime. Wait, where are we meeting?"

"Want to meet at my place?" Sara asks.

"Sounds good to me!"

"Awesome, let's say seven thirty. Bring beer and wine, and I'll order pizza."

"Perfect!" we all say in unison. I can't wait to hang out with the girls tonight. It's been too long, and it's the first time that we can get together and just chat and catch up without any drama hanging over our heads. Liam and I are so good right now. Sherri and Mark are in their gross honeymoon phase, but I'm loving it more than a little bit. It's so good to see Mark happy again; he didn't seem unhappy anymore, but this, this is next level. I think he's falling for Sherri, and I think she's totally worth it. Sara is a bit of a closed book lately but maybe that will change tonight, or maybe she really is just too busy with work to think about a man. Either way, I'm looking forward to it. My phone pings a text message tone.

Liam: *Hey, hun, plans tonight? You're running out of time to catch all the Hallmark movies before Christmas, and my couch is calling your name. *Winky face**

Jenna: *Can we catch up on them tomorrow night? I just made plans with*

Sherri and Sara for pizza and wine! I miss you, but I did just spend the entire night and morning with you. I think I might miss them more. Hahaha. Just kidding!

Liam: *You are totally not kidding. My couch will still be here tomorrow, and so will Hallmark. Have a great time! Maybe I'll con Mark and Noah into Christmas shopping.*

Jenna: *Oooh, my list of books I want is tucked under your keyboard in your office. They're all on your front table for your easy shopping experience.*

Liam: *Jenna! I am not just buying you books from my own store for Christmas!*

Jenna: *Suit yourself, it could've been that easy*

Liam: *You're crazy, have fun tonight. I love you.*

Jenna: *I love you too.*

I'm still smiling when I walk down the street to my car that's parked in front of Jenna's Blooms. I climb into my driver's seat and can't help but look up at my storefront through my windshield. How cool is this? I have my very own flower shop, and I'm buying my own house. I'm in love with the best man I could ever imagine. My family is here, happy and healthy, and Christmas is next week! Tears of joy are shimmering in my eyes when I catch my reflection in my rearview mirror. I wipe at them before they can fall, but I sit in the joy for a minute. The gratefulness. I am so blessed to be given everything that I have. I whisper a prayer of thanks to Amy and promise her that I will cherish every second.

Sometimes, it feels like she's missing so much; so much time has passed, and life keeps moving forward. But I try to tell myself she's not missing it; we're missing her, but she's been right here with us through it all. The good and the bad, she's got our backs, like our own personal guardian angel. I can feel her happiness when I'm playing with Andi, and I know she's smiling down on Mark finding love again with Sherri. Heaven only knows what she thinks of Liam and me, but I know she must be loving it, the family being joined in so many ways that we can never be parted now. I wipe my eyes again and head home to get ready for our girl's night in,

The Holiday is playing in the background on the TV, we are all sitting on the floor with pillows everywhere, each with a glass of wine and two cheesy pizzas strewn around us.

"Could this night *be* any more perfect?" Friends-isms have started to make up the general gist of our relationships. We've assigned ourselves corresponding roles to all the characters on the show. I am Monica because Sherri says Liam, and I remind her of Chandler and Monica by how opposite we are. Sherri got Phoebe because she's so eccentric and hilarious, and Sara is Rachel because that was all that was left. She isn't actually anything like Rachel; she's the least self-centred person of us all; she is passionate about her job like Rachel was, but is also way more focused on her family than her job, whereas Rachel pretty much left her whole family for her 'friend family' and later to focus on her career. The guys are a bit tougher: Liam got Chandler because I got Monica, Noah is a given to be Joey because his evening exploits precede him, and he's so charmingly funny, Mark being Ross isn't a great match, but he's the only one of us with a kid, so it works. He's way cooler than Ross and not as funny, to be honest, but hey, we can't all be winners.

"So, how long do you think you'll be in your own house before Liam kidnaps you and puts a ring on it?" Sherri does not hold back. I almost spew my wine all over us all but gather my wits and say, "I'm not sure. We haven't talked much about the timeline. I feel a bit like we just got this whole communication thing sorted out with what each of us is wanting from the other. It feels like piling on to think or talk about the timeline of it all. I mean, if I'm honest, he could ask me to marry him tomorrow, and I wouldn't say no, but that doesn't mean I will move in with him tomorrow or marry him next week."

"Can I just say that I love how you're sticking to your guns with him? It is so sweet that he's stepping back, but it's also like, why is that sweet? He should be able to give you the time and space you need to reach your goals without getting a medal. Sometimes we expect so little from men, and I'm so proud of you for expecting just enough."

My face warms at Sara's praise; she's not wrong, though, "Thanks, Sara, that means so much coming from you, especially being the sister of the man in question."

"I mean all men, though. We give them too much leeway to treat us less than, and they don't mean to, and it doesn't mean they love us less, but whatever we allow will occur. You're an example to us all, Jen."

Sherri lifts her glass, "I'll toast to that."

We all clink our glasses as Sherri adds, "Though I will say I won the lottery with *your* brother!" She points her glass in my direction, "He is the most kind-hearted and attentive boyfriend I've ever had. Even with you causing my bar to be higher, he is soaring. And oh my god, the way he is with Andi melts my heart every single time I see them together. She is such his little princess, and she just adores him, like he made the world for her."

"It doesn't make you jealous at all that he has to give so much time and attention to her?" I don't ask this as a trick question; I genuinely don't know how I would handle having to share a new love, even if it is with the cutest little six-year-old.

Sherri thinks about it for a few moments, but then a genuine smile spreads across her face, "No. Honestly, she is the best thing that ever happened to him, and I see his heartbreak from the past, and I see Andi's, and I want nothing more than to soothe it even just a little bit. I know you meant sharing him with Andi, but sometimes I also consider that I'm sharing him with Amy too, the memory of her anyways," she glances over at Sara to gauge how touchy this will be, I'm guessing, but Sara just smiles and waves her to go on. "I mean, it's hard to explain, but in a way, I'm sharing all of you with her. She is still such a huge part of this town and this family; there's no chance I would want to undo that or replace that. Everything I've learned about her tells me I would love her too, so I can't hate her just because we fell in love with the same guy. I just want to do right by her. By all of you. Mark and Andria especially."

'Whoa, wait. In love with the same guy?"

"You're in love with my brother?" Sara and I yell at the same time. Sherri bursts out laughing, then covers her face with her hands while squealing. "YES!"

My heart swells at the joy on her face and the happiness that I know she brings to Mark and Andi's lives. She's right; she will never be Amy, but she's not even trying to be. She is just so perfectly *Sherri.*

After jumping up and down like middle schoolers, we settle back into our cocoons, "Okay Sara, what's next for you? Who do you have your eye on?"

"Oh, no one." We glare, and she yells, "For real, no one! I don't have time for a guy. You two and your romances occupy enough of my brain." She says it jokingly, but I sense a hint of something, she's holding back, I just don't know what.

"Come on, there must be someone. I've been back for three months, and I haven't seen you with anyone."

"Jenna, I spend all my time at work and my free time at the farm helping mom and dad or with Andi. There honestly just isn't time to even look around and see what the prospects are."

"What about Jack?" Sherri says. That grabs my attention. "Huh? Jack Turner? What about him?"

Is he a prospect for Sara? He owns the Christmas tree farm, creatively named Balsam Trees. He sells more than balsam fir trees I promise. I didn't know there was ever anything between him and Sara, but I guess I wasn't here for so long, and so many things kept popping up that I missed. Makes me wish I never left. That can't be helped now, though. I have to focus on the here and now!

I never really knew him that well, but I don't think I've seen him once since I've been back. Even though he hung out with Mark and Noah a lot in school, he must not spend too much time with them these days. I glance at Sara, about to ask her how old he is when I notice her blushing.

Wow! Okay, this is a thing then! Sara and Jack Turner? I raise one eyebrow at her. "Sara?"

She looks back and forth between us and finally gives in, "Okay, okay, there might have been a possibility of a thing, but it was a couple of years ago, and nothing happened, and now it's over, and I don't want to talk about it?"

I look at Sherri. "How did you know about this?"

"Oh, I almost had a thing with him too." She deadpans. My jaw drops, but she continues, "By almost, I mean, I wanted to. Have you seen him? He's walking, talking gorgeous on a stick with a side of sexy farm boy."

I burst out laughing again because, like I said, I don't know Jack that well, but I do remember that much! She nailed that description of him. Now Sara's neck and face are flaming red.

"So why almost? Why didn't you go for it?" I ask Sherri. Sara glares at me. Oh, there's definitely something I'm missing here, and I'm about to get all the tea, whether Sara likes it or not.

"He was into Sara. I didn't want to mess with that."

"Why are you so quiet about this?" I point at Sara. "And why are you so nonchalant about this?" I say, pointing at Sherri incredulously, "As if this isn't the biggest piece of gossip since I've been back…. That isn't about me!"

"It was nothing, that's why! He was into me? What does that even mean, Sherri? Just forget about it, Jenna. It was nothing."

"You keep saying that, but who are you trying to convince?" Sherri starts to speak again, and Sara levels her with narrowed eyes, but Sherri raises both her hands, "Hey, I just tell you what I know, I see a lot from behind that coffee counter. But this time, my Sara darling," she coos at Sara who gives her a scowl in return, "this time, he flat out told me. I came on strong, I was new in town and didn't know Sara well, other than she was my boss's sister, and Jack came in fairly often but never stayed. Unless..." she drags that word out like there's a secret coming, "Little miss Sara was somewhere in the shop, then he zeroed in and pulled up a seat."

"Oh, come on. We have been friends for years; he has been one of Noah's best friends since high school. You can't say because he sat with me for a coffee once in a while that he's 'into me,' as you put it."

Sherri waves her hand in front of her. "No, no, no, hold on. I thought that exactly...at first. Locals always join each other for coffee, so I wasn't going to let that stop me, but when I flat-out asked him out one day, he smiled his perfect smile - you know the one with the dimple on his right cheek? Anyways, he pointed over at where Sara was sitting...." Sara rolls her eyes now, so she's heard this before obviously. Sherri continues, "And said to me, 'I'm sorry, but that one sitting over there, she's making me wait, but she's the one for me.'"

"Oh my God! He did not say that. And give me a break, Sherri, even if he did, he was kidding."

Sherri mocks outrage. "What?" She runs her hands down both of her sides to her hips. We all burst out laughing, "He didn't want some of this? Seriously, Sara, he didn't have to lie to get out of going out with me, and he didn't lie, he only has eyes for you! Have you ever seen him with any other girl?"

I smile at them both. "I haven't seen him at all since I've been back. Where is he hiding out?"

Sara answers a little too quickly. "He's busy on the farm. You did come back right before Christmas, remember? Anyways, guys, it doesn't even matter. I don't see him that way. He did show interest once, but I shot him down. It'd be too weird; he's Noah's friend. It was rough for a bit, but we're finally getting back to how we were before, easy friendship. That's all I want right now. It's all I have time for."

"Oh yeah, it would be super weird. Liam and Mark aren't friends at all, so I have no idea what that might be like?" I deadpan, but I can't help my smile that follows. That earns me another scowl. "It's not the same; you and Liam were always destined for each other."

That surprises me coming from Sara. I mean, I always had a crush, and now I know he did too after high school, but always? "What do you mean we were always destined for each other?"

"He was always with us to be with you. It was so obvious, even when we were kids. He had his own friends that weren't in Noah and Mark's group, but you were so often with Mark and then later with Amy and me that Liam always found his way to hang with us all, too."

"I had no idea. Is that crazy? I was literally in love with him when I was ten years old, and I had no clue he even noticed my existence."

"Yeah, yeah, great love story." Sara smirks, showing me there's no heat behind her sarcasm. "Anyways, it's not like that with Jack. He's just always been a great friend, but there's never been anything more. End of story."

Sherri and I share a knowing look; we're all going over to Jack's together tomorrow for our Christmas trees. So, for now, we let the subject drop.

"I'm so excited that we all get to spend Christmas Day together at the farm. How cool is that? Andi is so excited! She said last year your parents gave her a horse."

Sara laughs. "Yes, they did. To be fair to them, she was already on the farm and unclaimed by anyone, so they just put a bow on her and told her she belonged to her."

I smile. picturing Andi's little face full of excitement to have her own horse, "Every little girl's dream."

"It definitely is. That's what we do with most of the time we spend together. I take her over there to groom Daisy or go on little rides around the farm with her. She's pretty good in the saddle, calm and sure handed. The kid has no fear." She shakes her head with a sad smile.

"Just like Amy, eh?"

Sara smiles. "Yeah, exactly. The only kid I know who could ride bareback at six years old and never fell off. I haven't had Andi on bareback yet, but I have no doubt she'll keep her seat just fine."

Sherri says quietly, "Will it be weird for your parents for me to be there? They've been so kind to me anytime I've been at the farm with Mark, but it's only been when we've been picking up Andi from a sleepover or dropping her off to ride with you. We don't want to make them uncomfortable."

I stay quiet and hope Sara has something to ease Sherri's worries. I don't know how any of this might feel for Mr. and Mrs. Ryan. I can see how it might be weird, but they are such wonderful people, and they love Mark like a son; I can't imagine them wanting anything but happiness for him.

Thankfully, Sara says just the right thing: "Oh Sherri, don't feel that way at all. They love Mark, and they love seeing him happy. It will always hurt that Amy isn't here, but it doesn't hurt more because you are. Having Andria in their lives has soothed so much of their grief, but it will never be gone completely. Please tell me you'll come to Christmas."

I can tell by the tears welling in Sherri's eyes that those are the words she needed to hear. "Of course, I will. I just wanted to be sure it wasn't just Mark thinking everything was okay there when it really wasn't."

"Men can be dumb sometimes, that is for sure. But no, in this case, Mark is super sensitive to my parents' grief. I think he's still trying to make up for being gone for those five years, not that anyone holds that against him. We all handle grief differently. He needed to be alone, but I was the opposite. I was planning to go to the city to write for a bigger newspaper or magazine, but I couldn't leave Mom and Dad after that. Not because they guilted me into staying; I just didn't want to miss a single day that I have to spend with them and to be here for them. They needed my support in their grief, but I needed them too. When Amy died, a part of me died.

And the closest people I have to understanding that are my parents and my brothers. I couldn't imagine walking through my day-to-day life in another city without that level of understanding of what's going on inside of me. I needed them, and that meant staying close. That's why I took the promotion at the paper, to make working there worth it."

I nod my head, more to myself than to them. "I get that. I know I left, too, but I do get why you didn't. Do you love working there now? I know you didn't before, but once you decided to stay, did that help?"

"You know," Sara says thoughtfully, "I really don't love it. It's fine, it pays the bills, and I'm not miserable, but if I'm honest, no, I don't love it."

"I thought you loved writing, though; you light up when you talk about some of the stories you cover."

"I do. Writing is my passion, but not for the newspaper. I want to write a novel. I want to write lots of novels. Actually, I have so many stories flying around inside my head. If I had the time, I would love to get them out into the world." Sara covers her face with both of her hands like she didn't mean to tell us all that. "It's just a dream; forget I said anything about that!"

Sherri laughs, "Ha! Amazing! Do it. What is stopping you? You don't have to quit the paper; just cut back your hours and dedicate time to writing for you."

"Easier said than done, Sherri. I don't see you chasing your dreams."

"Whoa, whoa, whoa! Sherri has dreams? Beyond making world-famous beverages for me every morning? What do they consist of?"

Sara answers while Sherri is the one sporting a glare now. This evening is turning out to be way more informative than I expected.

"Yes, Sherri wants to teach preschoolers. She doesn't have her college diploma in Early Childhood Education, but she worked in a daycare out west, and I've told her a million times to apply here and do the classes online while working for Liam."

"Um...yes, Sherri! Yes!" I can't contain my excitement. The thought of these two ladies, whom I get to call my best friends, chasing their dreams just like I did fills me with so much joy I could scream. Okay, maybe I am screaming, but I love this for them.

"How did I not know about any of this? Listen to me. We are doing this. I can talk to Liam, and he will give you any time off you need."

"No, Jenna, thank you. I can do that if I need to, but you are right," she looks over at Sara, "Let's do this, Sara! Let's make this happen. We are worth this." Sara agrees and smiles so big and so genuine that I can tell this is going to be good for her. She deserves to put herself first for once, and I can't wait to help them reach their goals the same way they've helped me!

We spend the next hour chatting about Christmas gifts and traditions and what everyone's doing this week leading up to Christmas. We restart The Holiday because none of us watched any of it the first time, even though we've all seen it a hundred times, it's our favourite! We snuggle into our pillow beds to watch, but we all doze off almost right away after so much wine and pizza. Just when I think I couldn't be any happier, I get a night like this to show me how truly blessed I am. No matter what pain and heartache life throws at us, we will rise together and find what lights us up.

CHAPTER

Eighteen

Liam

"Liam, when we get up there, grab those two old boys and put them out in the north paddock, then the mares will all fit in the barn for the night. I don't want any of them bellowing out here all night long." I'm at the farm today helping Dad and Noah wean the babies born this past spring. The cattle got done a couple of months ago, but he's late on the horses this year. Noah and I both took the day off to give him a hand. Sometimes, it takes more shuffling than it should, but the old man wants what the old man wants.

"Noah, for Christ's sake! Don't you have those panels set up yet? They're foals, not elephants; how secure do you think they need to be?" Dad isn't usually so on edge, but weaning always stresses him out. There isn't a lot that can go wrong. The way the farm is set up is pretty simple: we just lead each mare into a stall in the barn and leave all the babies here on the other side of the farm where they've been turned out all summer and fall. They make a little noise but it's mostly the mares that get worked up, but even they'll be over it in a day or two. We leave the foals where they are because they're harder to transport, and there's a large shelter in their paddock that they can stay warm in and eat hay to their heart's content all winter.

We're heading up to the other barn now to make sure the stalls are ready for the mares to move in. Once they're settled in up here, they'll get turned out to another paddock up this way to do the same thing for the winter until we bring them in to have their next foals and do this all again next year. There's another barn down close to the house that they keep all the riding horses in. These two 'old boys' that I'm walking out of the barn now used to be down there, but they've gotten to retire up here in the grassy heavens of the north paddock. Acres of grass all to themselves and warm stalls full of all the hay they can eat. In the winter months, they come in the barn at night, but they'll be okay out here for a few days. They shouldn't be out in the cold full-time like they used to, but this week is pretty mild as far as December weather goes. Noah and I used to ride these two all over this whole farm when we were kids. We named them John and Ron when we were about ten years old. Stupid kids that we were, poor horses.

I lead them from the barn down the short slope to the gate, one on either side of me, and they both nuzzle into my shoulder.

"Hi guys, are you getting kicked out by the ladies?" I rub each of their noses to show them I'm sorry for my part in it. "Not fair, is it? Don't worry, it's just for a few days, then you'll be back in your cozy beds."

They both knicker as I slide their halters off their ears and down their noses. Old John runs and kicks his hind feet out behind him like he's a yearling and Ron follows suit. I shake my head, saying, "Couple of idiots."

I make my way back to Dad and Noah; they're waiting in the RTV to head back down to grab the mares. There are six of them so we'll each have to make two trips. I slide into the back seat of the RTV and slap Noah on the shoulder. "You coming with us to Jack's tonight?"

"Nah, pretty sure I don't need to be a fifth wheel with you and Mark and your women."

"Hey, Sara's coming! Come on! Everyone needs a tree, even a Scrooge like you. It's not a double date or anything."

He shakes his head and laughs. "Sara's going? Jack'll love that. Does he know?"

I laugh. "Give that a rest. He's fine with her, and she seems fine too; let's not rock that boat, but all the more reason for you to come. She won't want to get stuck talking with him, and she doesn't need to feel like the fifth wheel either."

He scoffs. "Oh. Thought it wasn't like that?"

"Well, you know how Jack can be. I don't want her to feel pressured; he's too nice, and so is she. She'll feel obligated to visit with him. And besides, it's our first Christmas all of us back together again. You can't miss it. Jenna is so excited, and I want to make it special for her; for some reason, for her, that involves you being there."

He beams his megawatt smile at me. Yeah, jerk face, she does that to me too, but he replies with a wink, "Well, if Jenna wants me there, I'm there." There's no sarcasm in his tone whatsoever; he genuinely loves Jenna, and I love that they have a connection that has held up to the test of time from when we were kids.

He was always closer to Mark than I was, so I spent a lot more time at their house. In later years, I was usually just along for the ride to try to see Jenna, though no one knew that at the time. But I think she has always seen Noah as an extension of Mark, another big brother to look out for her, and I love that for her. For both of them.

Losing Amy took its toll on all of us in different ways, but being the oldest, it seemed to have hit Noah in a way I can never understand. Like we were his job, to take care of, to protect and always be there for and that when she died, he failed her somehow. I know I've felt that way too, and I also know it isn't true, so I can imagine he must know that too, but he always made us his responsibility, so I have a feeling it runs a little deeper for him. I think that's why he has let loose a little since she died, almost like it wasn't worth it to him. What's the point if we can lose our loved ones anyway? I hope he finds someone that means enough to him to start caring again. He's never stopped caring about all of us who were already here, but he hasn't let anyone new in, and I think sometime in the last six years, he's stopped caring about himself. He doesn't have any hopes for the future, to find love or to have a family because he knows it can all be ripped away from you in a second. We all know that, but I don't think he's made peace with that fact yet.

After we have all the mares moved and tucked into the barn for the night, I pop my head in the house to see Ma before I head home to shower and get ready to meet everyone over at Jack's farm.

I walk in and take my boots off. The kitchen smells like Christmas baking, and there's no better smell in the world. Mom is working over the island, rolling out dough for sugar cookies. I lean in and place a quick kiss on her cheek and steal a piece of dough at the same time; she's fast, though, and she smacks my hand with a smile. Fast enough to reprimand but not fast enough to keep it from my mouth.

"Mmmm.... So good, Ma..." I mumble while I chew the sweet and buttery dough.

"I thought you'd learn that if you want to keep your fingers, you'll keep them out of my cookie dough."

"I haven't lost one yet, so I think I'm winning." She smacks my shoulder as I walk around the island to pull up a stool, "I just came in to say hi and bye; I gotta run to get ready, but I wanted to see if there's anything else you need done before Christmas dinner on Monday."

"Oh, that's sweet, dear, but no, I think we're all set. I'm just so happy everyone is going to be here together. It's been so long." I glance at the counters and notice how many cookies she has cooling. "What is all this, Mom? You feeding an army with sugar cookies?"

"Ha! No, just your crew and little Andria. She's coming over to decorate them tomorrow and I wanted to make sure I have enough."

I shake my head and laugh. "Oh, I think you have enough mom, there's gotta be a hundred cookies here."

"Ninety-six actually but who's counting?" She smirks her cheeky grin with the same dimple that Noah sports when he's being an arse. "What's going on tonight that you have to get ready for?"

"We're all going over to Jack's to pick out Christmas trees. Jenna wanted to make it a family event." I look cautiously over at her to gauge her reaction to that. Christmas is still so sensitive for her. For all of us, but I think for her especially. She doesn't hint at being upset by the idea of us getting trees together, so I venture forward. "Want us to grab you guys a tree while we're there?"

"I would love that, Liam; pick one out that Amy would love, and Andria can decorate it tomorrow after she's finished with the cookies." I smile and place a kiss on the side of her head before I head for the door. "Will do, Ma."

I love how much we all talk about Amy, not exactly as if she's still here, because that would be weird, but not really like she's gone either. It still feels so much like she's just gone away. Like she might come back home in time to see the tree this year. We all know she isn't coming back, but I think the more we remember her and talk about her, the more it keeps her alive and her presence strong in our lives. Sometimes, it makes it hurt a little more, but sometimes, it just feels good to remember.

Noah and Dad are on their way in. As I get to my truck, I throw a wave over my shoulder and holler: "Five o'clock, Noah! See ya there!"

"Who knew getting a Christmas tree could be so romantic?" Sherri asks as we walk through the rows of trees, snow falling softly, and little white twinkle lights strung all throughout to set the mood.

"Have you never read a Christmas romcom? It's the most romantic Christmas activity out there! Jees Sherri, you work in a bookstore!" Sara chastises her properly because come on, even I know this, but then again, I make a point to read a bit of every genre that I'm selling, and she sticks to making the coffee.

She confirms my thoughts by saying, "Hey! I just make the coffee; I don't spend my days in the corner reading."

She gives Jenna a pointed look, who responds quickly with, "Hey, don't judge."

Noah grumbles something indecipherable behind us. I can't help but laugh to myself at him. He did get suckered into this romantic outing. Mark has his arm draped around Sherri's shoulders, and Andi holds his other hand as she skips along beside them. They are picture-perfect right now. I'm walking with my arm around Jenna's waist with her pulled in close to my side. Sara hangs back with Noah, and I feel a little bad that I was wrong about it feeling like a couple's thing because it definitely does.

In my defence, I wasn't wrong about everyone needing a tree; we all do, and I love that we're doing this together. Just like when we were kids. Noah, Mark and I all brought our trucks, and they're going to be loaded with trees when we leave here tonight.

"Hey, we didn't get hot chocolate!" Andi suddenly shouts from beside her dad.

Mark chuckles and pats her head. "Your reward comes after you do the hard work, honey. Didn't you bring your saw?"

Andi's eyes grow wide as she looks up at her dad. She quickly spins her head to look at me, and then her Uncle Noah, then back to her dad. She's clocking that none of us brought a saw to cut down the trees. I can see Noah out of the corner of my eye, trying to hold in his laughter. Sara elbows him, silently telling him to keep it together.

"Daddy? I didn't bring a saw. Why didn't you bring a saw?" She's talking slowly like she's trying to figure out if this is a joke, while she's also trying to figure out how we're getting trees without a saw, whether it's a joke or not.

"I don't know, Andi. I thought you were in charge this Christmas. I cut your tree down last Christmas."

"But you cut our tree down every Christmas!" She implores him.

"Well, all the more reason for you to take a turn., don't you think?" Mark is keeping a straight face amazingly well; he's used to this and apparently immune to her sad, puppy dog eyes, but this is killing the rest of us. I'd cut this girl down as many trees as she wanted if she looked at me like that for more than five seconds.

Oh, here we go. She's had enough of this. Her hands go to her hips, and she lifts her chin high and turns to face me... Whoa, wait, why me? I try to protect myself any way I know how... I step behind Jenna. That's right, I'm weak.

"Uncle Liam?" I hesitate but can't ignore her sweet little voice. "Yes, Andi?"

She flips her hand out to me, palm up. "Can I use your phone?" I hear Noah snickering behind, followed by a grunt and another elbow from Sara. *Thanks sis.* I look down at my niece, wondering what she's up to. "My phone Andi? Why do you need my phone?"

"Because..." She drags out the word, implying I should know what she's going to say next, but I'm at a loss. "I saw big chainsaws back at the tree shed, so I want to call Uncle Jack and ask him to bring me one. If Daddy can't use one of those, I know Uncle Jack will know how."

That does us all in. We all bend over laughing, holding our knees to keep from toppling over. Jenna and Sherri have tears in their eyes; Sara is high-fiving Andi, who looks confused about what's so funny. Mark finally catches his breath and lifts Andi up into his arms, looking her in the eyes with so much affection it almost hurts my chest to look at them. He says, "That, my girl, is exactly what we planned to do. You are so smart to think of that." He then kisses her cheek and flicks the top of her nose.

"You were going to call Uncle Jack all along?"

"Yeah, honey, we didn't want to carry a saw all the way back here because we have so many trees to choose from, so Uncle Jack said we can just call him when we find our trees, and he'll drive back with a chainsaw for us, and I will have you know, I do know how to use one of those big ones, thank you very much! Nobody cuts down a tree for my girl but me." He squeezes her tight, and she screams in delight. I notice now that Noah has brought his camera, and he snaps a perfect shot of our best friend with our niece. Jenna asks him to take one of the two of us, so we pose with the lights and trees behind us. Everyone gets in and makes funny faces. He sets the timer and sets the camera on a fence post so we can get some together. My heart has never been this full. There was a time when I didn't know if I would ever feel this way, days when sadness weighed me down, and I wondered how anything could be following a path that was meant to be. I still have days like that, but today isn't one of them. Today, I feel like I'm right where I'm supposed to be.

We wander through more rows of trees than I can count before one of the girls finally says, "This one!" Oh, did I say, finally said that? I *meant*, they finally say that and actually mean it. They each picked fifteen trees that all eventually weren't good enough. I think the romance is officially lost. Sara, Sherri and Jenna have run ahead with Andi and are calling to us to come see. Noah walks ahead and gets a picture of them with arms splayed, pointing to the perfect tree.

"Who's this one for?" Mark asks. Damn, why did we think all of us getting trees together was a good idea? We're going to be here until midnight.

"This one is mine!" Sara calls over to us. At the same time Andi throws herself on the one right beside and starts yelling, "Daddy, Daddy! I want this one! It has to be mine because it lives right beside Auntie Sara's!"

Mark laughs and says, "Can't argue with that logic! Noah, why don't you give Jack a call to bring the saw, and maybe that'll get these two to pick up the pace and choose theirs," he points to Sherri and Jenna as they discuss the various trees surrounding us.

Sherri scowls at him but leaves Jenna where they were looking, to look at another row over by Mark and Noah.

I'm being a creeper again. I can't help it, though. I move so I'm just out of sight behind a huge Christmas tree, watching Jenna examine each one she walks by. The little white lights that are strung overhead are making her eyes sparkle more than usual, and her cheeks are rosy from the cold. She's so fucking beautiful, and she's all mine. As she's about to walk by, I grab her wrist and pull her into me so we're both out of view behind this monster tree. She yelps in surprise, but I silence her by placing my mouth over hers. My lips form perfectly around hers like we were made for each other. I only have to nudge once with my tongue, and she opens for me, so perfect for me, always ready. Her hands are in my hair now, and I can't stop mine from roaming underneath her big winter jacket. Screw this cold weather. I feel like I've just come out of a sauna now that she's in my arms.

"Too many layers," I mumble against her mouth. She breaks away from me and laughs. She smacks my hand away from where it's pressed against her stomach. "Do you know how cold it is out here?"

"I can think of some ways to warm you up in a hurry." She smacks my chest playfully and chastises me. "Liam! This is a family establishment, jeez! 'Merry Christmas, kids, sorry for the show!'" I burst out laughing because she's not wrong, but I also don't give a shit. I'd take her anywhere she'd let me. Although I must admit it's not ideal that our brothers and my sister and niece are right around the corner, that doesn't stop me from kissing her again, though, until I hear the shutter of Noah's camera and his disgusted, "Get a room!"

Jenna pulls away, raises an eyebrow at me and says, "See, family establishment, your whole family is here." Noah laughs as he heads back to where everyone is greeting Jack. I turn back to Jenna. "Okay, okay, I'll keep my hands to myself if you pick a Christmas tree in the next five minutes."

"Done. I want this one!" She points behind me. I jerk my thumb over my shoulder at the aforementioned monster tree that's standing behind me. "This one?"

"Yup, it's perfect! And now it has memories already attached to it, we made out behind it, and Noah has a photo of us with it already, so it's the one!" My eyes widen. "Babe, I don't even know if this will fit in my house, it's gotta be twelve feet tall."

"Your living room is sunken and has vaulted ceilings. Don't even get me started on how big of a tree we could fit in there. This is the one!" She's not wrong. I've just never had a tree this big, but it will fit. Our first Christmas tree. A fucking monster. Here we go.

"Alright, go tell Jack." She runs over to them, yipping and clapping her hands like an overexcited toddler, and the smile spreading across my face is so big it hurts; her happiness is contagious. It's the first of many Christmases together, but this one feels extra special for some reason. The simplicity of it maybe we aren't married or worried about starting a family. We don't even live together yet, but her mom has a fake tree, and she doesn't have her house yet, so we decided to celebrate together at mine. So, this big ass tree right here is ours, and I love it.

Jack cuts everyone's trees, and we all choose one together for Mom and Dad, one perfectly Amy, not too tall, not too short, but a little fatter around the middle than you would expect to be considered perfect, just about to cross the line from pretty to awkward. She was very particular about her trees. Andi loves picking out a tree that her mama would've chosen and can't stop talking about decorating it tomorrow with Grandma.

She rides ahead with Jack and Sara in his RTV to get a head start on bagging the trees and getting her some hot chocolate. I don't know where Noah disappeared to, but it's nice to walk quietly through this winter wonderland with the love of my life by my side.

"Look at those two," she whispers into my ear.

"Jenna, no offence to your brother, but I'm not looking at what he's doing with his girlfriend when I have this beautiful woman on my arm right here."

"Oh okay, sweet talker," she rolls her eyes at me, "I just mean, look at how happy they are. Aren't they so great together?"

She's not wrong. I've noticed a huge change in Mark since he started seeing Sherri. He's happier than he's been in six years, and yeah, sometimes, if I think on that too long, it hurts a little, but seeing him like this, with Sherri and Andi and finally looking whole again, it feels too good to feel bad about it. "They are, hun; you're right. I'm happy for them. I'm happy for us, too."

She leans her head on my shoulder as we walk hand in hand, and I know I will never be anything but the happiest man alive with this woman by my side.

CHAPTER

Nineteen

Jenna

"Will you just turn it to the left a little bit? There's this huge bare spot right here that I don't want to have to look at every day. I don't think it's even straight; it's definitely leaning. Liam! Ugh! Can you hear me?"

He grumbles quietly, but not quietly enough that I can't hear him, of course. Passive aggressive much? "Oh, I hear you. I'm about ready to throw this damn tree out the fucking window; that's what I'm hearing." Or not... Just generally aggressive then, okay. I throw my hands up but put on my best pouty face. "Come on! Why do you have to be like this? I'm trying to make this special for us, I just want it to be perfect, and all you can do is bitch and complain that the tree is too big?"

"Jenna, all you have done since we got home is bitch and complain that I'm not doing it right! Doing what right? It's a fucking Christmas tree; put it in the stand and add water and ornaments. You are making this into a shitshow that it doesn't need to be!"

"I am making this into a shitshow? If your Christmases were so much better in the past without me, then I'll just leave." This man is the most infuriating man I've ever met! Why can't he just do what I ask with a fucking smile? It's Christmas! Our first Christmas together, I just want everything to be perfect, and he throws it back in my face like I'm a pain in his ass, well fuck him. I don't have to be here doing this. I wanted to spend this time together, but not at the expense of our relationship. I spin on my heel and head for the door; I hear him scramble with the unfastened tree.

"Jenna, wait. No... Argh... What the fuck.... This fucking tree... Jenna!"

I can't help but smile to myself, not because I enjoy his misery but because listening to him fight a twelve-foot Christmas tree is kinda funny. Okay, so maybe I'm enjoying his misery a little bit. He calls out again, "Jenna, please, you can't leave me here like this!"

I stand quietly by the door, just out of his sight line.

"Jenna!"

I don't answer.

"For fuck's sake, I'm being held hostage by a Christmas tree!"

That gets me. I can't hold in my giggles any longer.

"Jenna..." He growls from the living room; his voice is low and rumbly and makes my stomach flip a little. "Are you laughing at me right now?"

I squeak. "No."

"Jenna." That growl again. Ugh, how is he so sexy even when he's being a total ass. "Get your ass back in here and hold up this damn tree while I fasten it in."

"Or what?"

"Or I'm going to drop this monster of a tree and destroy all your beautiful decorating in here and come after you to throw you over my shoulder and make sure you know you're not leaving this house tonight."

Heat runs through my whole body at that thought. "That's not making me want to come to help you. What happens if I come back willingly?"

He huffs a laugh; he knows he's got me right where he wants me. "Get in here and find out."

After securing the tree and sufficiently making up for our fight, we make our way back to the living room to decorate! This is my favourite part, but I agree to leave him to do the lights while I make popcorn and hot chocolates because we don't have time to make up after another fight before we have to go meet everyone at the coffee shop for last-minute Christmas shopping.

I am standing in the kitchen making hot chocolate, with a flush to my cheeks, when he comes up behind me and wraps his arms around my waist. "What are you thinking about?"

"Oh, nothing..." I draw out the last word to tease him a little. He kisses me behind my ear and buries his face in my hair at the crook of my neck. I lean into him and moan a little while arguing at the same time. "Liam, we have to get this done; we're meeting everyone to go shopping at three."

"I know, I know." He groans. "Sometimes I can't wait until Christmas is over to have you all to myself again. There's so much going on this week that involves us leaving this house. I'm not really here for it." I smack him gently and laugh. "Soon enough, my love, now let's get the tree done! I have snacks, they'll give you sustenance to carry on."

"It'll give me something, but I don't know if that's the sustenance I'm looking for right now."

I smack him again as I walk past him on my way to turn my monster tree into a masterpiece.

It's finally Christmas Day!

This whole Christmas season has been a dream. I seriously couldn't have hoped for more for my first Christmas back. It's so hard to believe that a few short months ago, I was sitting alone in my apartment in Toronto. I wasn't wrong; being surrounded by love and family is exactly what I needed to get my life on the track I had always hoped for.

Liam and I have just picked up my mom, and we're headed to the farm for Christmas dinner with the whole Ryan crew. We walk through the door, and Andria is instantly in my arms and reaching across to my mom. "Auntie Jenna! Gran! You're finally here!"

I don't know how early Mark got over here with her, but she acts like she's been waiting for us since she got up this morning. "Hey, baby girl." Liam coos and pries her off my neck to swing her around in a circle and into his arms, "Merry Christmas!" he says, then whispers something into her ear, and she giggles; my heart sings at the sight of the two of them.

Mark calls from the other room. "Andi! Come on, let them come in and sit down. You're not a very good door lady if your guests can't get in the house."

She rolls her eyes and drags us into the living room to see everyone. Andi assigns us our seats for gift-giving and continues to hop around the room in excitement. When I was a kid, we ate before gifts, but apparently, grandchildren get special privileges, and rules have changed. Fine by me. I'll always vote for gifts sooner. Everyone's swapping Christmas morning stories, but I notice someone's missing. "Hey, where's Noah?"

I direct my question to Mark because he talks to Noah the most. They work together at the fire station, but they also live next door to each other on the eastern edge of the farm; they've always been the closest of the three guys, so I expect him to know more than the others. He's sitting on the couch with his arm slung around Sherri but shrugs his one shoulder. "I don't know, his truck wasn't home when we left. We assumed he was here."

As if on cue, there's a knock on the door. "Why is he knocking at your parent's house?" I laugh as I get up to get to the door. As I reach to open the large wooden door to the Ryan's home, it occurs to me that this likely isn't Noah. I don't know why I didn't consider that before, but for some reason, a feeling of dread settles in my stomach. But it's Christmas day; what am I worrying about? Everyone's here that matters, so we're good.

Except Noah. Shit.

My fingers are wrapped around the knob, but I can't make myself pull. What if it's bad news on the other side of this door? I can't be the reason

Mr. and Mrs. Ryan have to deal with more grief. I can't be the one to open this door. Another knock sounds, and I nearly yelp in surprise. Mark calls from the living room, but I can tell he's heading this way, "Jenna, did you get lost? Open the door!"

I turn the knob and pull it open, but for all the worry getting me to this point, nothing could have prepared me for what I see on the other side.

"Dad?"

"Dad!" Mark's voice behind me doesn't have the surprise or the question in it that mine does. I blink rapidly, trying to make sense of what I'm seeing. "What are you doing here? How did you know we were here?"

"Jenna, hold on; I invited him. Dad, come in. The Ryan's are expecting you. I just didn't get around to telling Jenna."

I look at him incredulously. "What?" I am stunned. I should have more to say than that, but I don't. Mark invited our dad to Christmas dinner at the Ryan's? Mark talks to our dad? What will Mom say to this? Oh my God, Mom! She's going to be shell-shocked over this. Fuck, I'm shell-shocked over this, and he wasn't my husband who left me to raise two teenagers on my own without a backward glance. Has she even seen him in the last twelve years?

I know I haven't. What is he doing here? Oh shit, I can't catch my breath. They're coming too quick, and I can't get one to go deep enough. My face feels wet. Am I crying?

"Fuck, Jenna! Are you okay? Jenna, breathe!"

I can hear the panic in Mark's voice, but I can't worry about that right now.

"Li—Liam..." I manage to choke out. I need Liam; he's my safe place. I need air. I need space. I try to get past my dad to get out the door, but nobody is moving; no one understands, ugh! Where is Liam? No one but him even knows that I can lose it like this.

"Babe, I'm here, breathe." His arms wrap around me and we're outside in seconds.

"I can't, Liam, I can't breathe." I try to inhale, but it's not working, "I'm so hot. Why is he here? Why did Mark keep this from me?"

"Ssshh, it's okay, Jenny girl, don't worry about them, just breathe, it's cold out here, let the air in, babe, you can do it." He's rubbing my back and stroking my hair. He is everything. I slowly count my breaths in and then out. I look up at him, and my eyes fill with tears again.

"Thank you."

"Don't thank me, Jen, just relax; you're okay." We stand together for minutes; I don't know how many.

"I couldn't catch my breath. Seeing Dad standing there just sent me back to those days when he first left, the nights crying, waiting for him to come back. It all came flooding back, and I couldn't stop it. I just knew I needed you to hold me. I tried to tell Mark to get you." I'm talking faster than I can think, but I am getting air in my lungs now. I'm starting to feel better.

"Ssshhh, it's okay. He called for me; I was coming for you anyway. It's okay, we're okay."

"I have to go back in there."

"No, you don't. You don't have to do anything."

"Well, I'm actually really cold now, and I want to know what the fuck is going on, and my mom is going to freak, so I want to go back in there, though I wish I didn't."

"Let me know what you need from me, hun; I'll follow your lead. We can walk right out of here."

"Liam, this is your family's Christmas dinner, and my first time being a part of it; we aren't going anywhere; if anyone is, then my dad can leave." I reach past him to open the door and find the entryway now empty. Liam comes in behind me and wraps my hand in his. He is my courage. My emotions run so wild, but he grounds me. I can handle this. I can handle anything as long as I have him with me. In the living room, everyone is seated around the room, with my dad on the couch beside Mark, talking animatedly with Andria. Okay, now, for real, what the actual fuck? Why is Andi acting like she knows our dad?

"Mark? What is going on? Why is he here?" He turns to me, "Jenna! Hey, are you okay?" He stands to come to me, but I put my hands up. "I'm fine. I just lost it there for a second. It happens sometimes. I'm fine. Now tell me what this is all about?" I wave my hand aggressively in my dad's direction. I notice my mom now for the first time; she's sitting in the corner of the room in a big double-seater chair with her feet tucked up beneath her, but she doesn't look upset. She looks worried, but for me, she's not looking at my dad; she's staring at me.

"Mom? Did you know he was coming today?"

"Yes, dear, I knew. Mark just told me yesterday. I told him he should tell you, but if it wasn't going to go well, he didn't want it to ruin your morning with Liam." I whip my head around to look at Mark. "If it wasn't going to go well? How could this go well?" My voice is bordering on hysterical now. How could he do this? Why? I don't understand why.

"Let me explain; I reconnected with Dad out west a few years back. We've kept in touch and met up quite a few times. I wanted Andi to have a chance to know her grandfather, and to be honest, I wasn't opposed to getting to know my dad as an adult. He's not the horrible human you think he is, Jen."

He looks apologetically towards my dad. Screw that! He is a horrible person; he left his wife and two kids, for Christ's sake! For what?! No one even knows because he never called or came back to visit. I literally have not seen the man who supposedly raised me since I was ten years old.

Mark must be able to see my thoughts splaying across my face because he says, "Jenna, just hear us out. He fucked up, but haven't we all at some point?"

"Umm, okay, can't say I ever have quite to the extent he did, but sure, I'll give you that one."

Mark looks at my dad, but it's my mom who speaks to him. "John, why don't you tell Jenna where you've been and what you've been doing? There's no excuse for your poor choices; we know this much already from all our talks, but there is an explanation." She looks at me and says, "Those are not the same thing, my girl. There is no excuse for him leaving you, for leaving all of us, but he can explain, and you can try to understand."

"Here? Now? At the Ryan's family Christmas? Are we serious right now? Mark, what were you thinking? What were any of you thinking?" I let my eyes wander over the various Ryan family members throughout the room. Noah arrived at some point; I don't even know when, but he obviously avoided my drama on the front porch. Liam is still holding my hand; Sara is sitting with her parents on the couch opposite Mark and my dad. My cheeks flush in embarrassment. "Guys, I'm so sorry. This must be just crazy to you. We'll go. This is nuts." I shake my head. "I'm so sorry."

Liam squeezes my hand and whispers, "It's okay; you can do this here. Don't worry about everyone else. We can go to the office and talk, and if you want to leave before dinner, we can."

I look at his parents, and they nod their agreement.

Okay, I guess we're doing this. Rehashing years of hurt and resentment on fucking Christmas Day. Let's go.

I look at Mark and my dad; to Mark, I say, "Alright, I'll hear him out. Liam said we can go to the office so Christmas can carry on for everyone else. I'm sorry again, guys." They all respond with waves and encouragement to take our time, as we head down the hall to Mr. Ryan's office.

"Okay, *Dad...*" I emphasize the 'dad' to prove a point. "What's your story? Why did you pack up and leave us 12 years ago and never contact us again? Oh, I'm sorry. I mean, never contact me again; you've been chatting with Mom and Mark this whole time, apparently."

"Now Jenna, it's not like that—" Mark cuts off my dad and says, "Jenna, I sought him out. I found out he was out west from a friend of a friend who does P.I stuff. You can hold everything else against him, but not that; I wanted to talk to him and make amends. After Amy died, I was so full of hate and anger it almost consumed me. The only bright thing in my life was Andria, and she is why I got out of bed every day. She reminds me every day that I am alive! That there are people that love me, that are still alive too! I had to forgive God for taking my wife, and I had to forgive myself for not being able to save her, for putting her in the position she was in, giving birth to my child. Next on my list was forgiving Dad for leaving us. That had nothing to do with Amy but everything to do with me. I needed peace. So, I found him, we got together and talked, and to make a long story short, I forgave him. I got my dad back, and Andi gained another grandfather."

My heart softens to Mark as he's talking. When did he get so wise? I agree with my mom that there's no excuse, but Mark is helping me see there may be a benefit to the explanation. I don't need to do this for him, but maybe I can get some resolution for myself and work towards healing. Lord knows this family has been through enough that we don't need to hang on to extra.

"Okay, Dad, I'm listening."

"First of all, Jenna, I want to say what a beautiful woman you've grown up to be. I can tell already by watching you since I got here that you are every bit the confident spitfire that you were already becoming at age 12. I'm so happy you haven't let life bring you down and suck that out of you. Mark has told me so much about your life and everything you've made of it."

I don't know what to say to that, thanks, I guess. I mean, he's not wrong; I've worked my ass off to become the woman I am today, I didn't do it alone, but it's nice of him to acknowledge and recognize my character. I don't think I'll give him that, though, so I just sit quietly, staring at him, waiting for him to tell his story. He coughs a little to clear his throat, then goes on, "What your brother said is true. I didn't seek him out. I wouldn't have done that and not reached out to you. I know I had many years since I reconnected with him that I could have called you yet didn't. If I'm honest, I was a coward. I didn't want to face your rejection; if I left it that I had never tried, then I could pretend you would have forgiven me if only I had reached out."

I nod to acknowledge that he should continue. Thankfully, he doesn't seem to expect too much from me right now, which is great because I don't have much to give. I rub my thumb along the top of Liam's hand, so grateful he's here. My dad continues. "After Mark moved back to Balsam River last year, I called your mom to clear the air and make peace so that I could come to town to see Mark and Andi if I wanted. I didn't want to cause any animosity in the family."

"Wait, you spoke to mom a year ago?"

"Yes." He glances in my mom's direction, and she smiles back warmly. Wow, this keeps getting better and better. The whole family is just living a lie while I smile and wave.

I rub my face with my hands and mumble, "Fuckin' hell. Okay, carry on."

He winces at my choice of language, and that almost makes me want to laugh. I'm twenty-four years old, Dad, not ten.

"I don't have any terrible sob story that is going to make you wish I never left. I didn't beat cancer; I didn't get blackmailed. I didn't cheat on your mother either; there's never been anyone else. I don't know, but maybe what I did was worse. I had a gambling addiction, Jenna. Bad. I spent every dime I'd made and then some. Your mother found out and gave me more chances than I ever deserved, and then she finally asked for a divorce. I had lost the car and our life savings and taken out multiple lines of credit. I took everything from her, everything except you two kids and the home that you lived in. If I divorced her, she would've lost the house to pay her half of my debt. There was no way that I could even begin to make things right for you all except leave. I never learned to quit while I was ahead, but I'd be damned if I was going to let my mistakes ruin your lives. I know you think my leaving ruined your life, but Jenna, my girl, you were better off without me. Look at you. Look at everything you've become. That's from your mama. She did right by you, and I knew Mark would always watch out for you."

I don't even bother to wipe the tears running down my face. I can't believe that after all these years, I have answers. Now I know why. There was a reason, and it had nothing to do with me. It was him. It was all him. "I don't know what to say. I don't think you know how much I blamed myself for you leaving; I don't know how to undo all that self-doubt and resentment just because I know now it wasn't me; it was you."

He leans forward in his seat to take my hand, but I hold tightly to Liam's; he says, "Jenna, honey, it could never have been you. I'm so sorry you felt that way. I wish I could go back and undo it, if not the gambling and the debt, then at least the unknown that you had to live with. I am so sorry."

"Why didn't you just explain...at the time? Why did you just leave without a word?"

"I wanted you to hate me so it wouldn't hurt so bad that I couldn't be there with you."

"Dad, hating you hurt. It hurt more than anything. It hurt so bad that Mark had to find you to heal that wound before he could move forward after his wife died!"

"I know that now. I'm so sorry. I'm sorry I didn't have the courage to speak to you sooner. I'm sorry I asked Mark and your mom to keep you in the dark. I truly thought it was what was best for you. I should never have thought to know what was best for you, though. I can't promise that I will never screw up again. All I can promise is that I'm a better man than I was then, and I'm here now, so I will talk to you. I will be honest every day, and I will try my best to deserve your forgiveness, whether you give it or not."

"What about the gambling?"

"Mark got me into a rehab centre and found me a great group of recovered addicts. I've been out of it for three years." Mark smiles at me and stands up to come crouch in front of my chair. "Jenna, please look into your heart and find the forgiveness that I know is in there. We've been through too much to hold grudges. He's paid his dues; let's live the life we have with all the love we've been given. Come on, sis."

We stand together, and he pulls me into a hug. My tears aren't just running down my face; now I'm openly sobbing. My dad stands tentatively watching Mark and me, unsure of what he should do next. I pull away from Mark and step toward him. I open my arms, and he wraps his around me. My God, it's been so many years since I've had a hug from my dad.

I pull away and wipe my eyes. "This doesn't undo the hurt, but I can recognize that you're a better man now. I believe you when you say you're sorry, so I will open my mind and my heart; I would love to get to know you again and work toward forgiving you."

His smile lights up his whole face. Mark's smile, I don't think I remembered that from when I was a kid. They look so much alike. He reaches for my hand and says, "That's all I ask for, my girl, just time and a chance to spend it with you both." He looks over to Mark and mouths, 'thank you.'

Mark comes up behind me and rubs the hair on the top of my head to make a mess of it. Ugh, what a jerk.

"What about me? Am I forgiven?" He makes his best puppy dog face.

"Um, no, you will have to wait, you big jerk! I need turkey first. Are we missing dinner?"

Liam laughs and says, "Not yet. Noah texted he was going to eat his left arm if you didn't hurry up, though."

"Why are both of our brothers so awful? Seriously, it's a wonder we survived dealing with them all these years."

"It really is. Let's go put him out of his misery." Tentatively, but laughing, we all go out to meet everyone in the kitchen. They're all sitting waiting, most likely holding their breath until they know how things are going to fall. Andi breaks the silence, of course, and asks, "Is grandpa staying for turkey? I set him a place beside me!"

My mom smiles and pats her head. "Of course he is, dear. Thank you for waiting for us." All at once, everyone breathes a sigh of relief, and the regular Ryan/Davis chatter resumes. What a day this turned out to be. Today is just another reminder of how much can change in twenty-four hours. Nothing is really as it seems when we have no real control over how our lives play out in the end.

I'm counting my blessings because even amongst our heartache, we are left with so much love at this table.

It is still the Merry Christmas that I had hoped it would be.

CHAPTER

Twenty

Jenna

"Liam, when was the last time you rode a horse?" He laughs from the other side of the mare that I'm grooming. "You don't want to know, but I can guarantee it's more recent than you, so I don't want to hear any mocking from you."

He comes around the front of Daisy's head and smacks my ass. Hard. "Ouch! What was that for?"

"Just getting you ready for the ride."

"What does smacking my ass do to prepare me for a trail ride?"

His laugh comes from the tack room now. "Nothing, I just wanted to touch your ass."

My cheeks flush, and not from the cold. "You're shameless."

He comes out with a saddle and bridle for my mare. I take them from him while he goes back for his own. I'm riding Andi's mare, Daisy, and he's riding a gelding they call Max. They both seem super chill, and that's a good thing because it's been some time since I've sat in a saddle. I know Daisy will take care of me. If she can take care of Andi, then I'll trust her with my minimal and outdated skills. Liam used to ride every day with Noah and their dad, moving cattle and just working the farm in general, so I'm sure even if it's been a year or two, he'll still ride better than I did when I was fifteen and rode weekly.

We finish tacking up and lead both horses out of the barn, into the cold. The sun is shining so brightly off the snow that it's almost blinding. I pull my sunglasses down off my head to cover my eyes and look behind me at Liam. "You ready for this old man?"

"Oh, don't 'old man' me! Let's see if you can still get on without a mounting block." Shit, I walked right into that one. We used to always cut up the riders that came out to the farm and had to use a mounting block to get on their horses. Easy for teenagers to make fun of 'oldies' in their twenties and thirties not being flexible enough to swing their legs over the back of the horse.

I adjust my jeans to optimize my chances, say a little prayer, and reach my hands up to hold the reins and horn in one hand and the back lip of the saddle in the other. I place the toe of my left boot in the stirrup and bounce on the toes of my right foot to get some leverage and hope for the best! I heave myself up and not so gracefully throw my right leg over the horse to settle my toes in the stirrup on the other side and plop my ass down in the saddle.

"Ha! I did it!" Liam's laughing but with no condescension. "You sure did, babe! Good on you!" He pauses for a second as he very gracefully steps into the stirrup, swings his leg over, and eases down into his saddle gently. Ugh, jerk. Then he says, "But you weren't sure if you could make it, were you?"

I wink at him. "I'll never tell." We both lift our reins and gently tap our horses' sides with our heels to tell them to take us to the trail that follows the border around the farm.

"Why did we wait for the coldest day of the year to do this?" Liam asks while blowing into his hands to warm them. Of course, he can ride with no hands. There was a time I could, too, but today, my fingers will freeze wrapped around my reins.

"I don't know. It sounded like a good idea, in theory. The sun shining on the snowy trees, beautiful horses, beautiful views, seemed like a romantic Christmasy activity."

He laughs, "I get the best view every day without the snow and horses."

"Ha-ha, sweet talker." I tease him, but the cold is hiding my blush. He is always saying sweet things like that, and I don't know if I'll ever get used to it. He melts my heart every day.

"Seriously though, when Mark said he rides out here with Andi, I was surprised but then thought, what a great thing to do on these days of nothingness between Christmas and New Year's. It is pretty damn cold though, isn't it?"

"Want to stop and build a fire? We haven't done that since high school, but without any whiskey to warm us up quickly, I'll have to get creative." He winks at me, and I roll my eyes at him.

"As romantic as that sounds, for real, I think I would rather just shorten this ride and head back to the house for some Bailey's in our coffees and sit at the fire that's indoors. I don't have the tolerance to this cold that I had back then." He laughs quietly, and his eyes drift away a little, in memory, I think. "Ya, you had stamina; you would've slept out here if I let you. I had to tell you stories of wolves and bears to save you from freezing to death. Thank God you never realized the bears are hibernating in December and the wolves wouldn't come near your fire. But you definitely would have got hypothermia, and Sara and Amy would've blamed Mark and Noah and I for allowing you to stay."

I bark a laugh at that memory. He's not wrong. I was so dumb. Just wanted to be brave and cool for the older guys. Mark made fun of me relentlessly, so I never accomplished much in that department anyway. Although, when I look at the guy on the pretty horse beside me, it looks like I'm winning. We turn the horses around to head back to the barn rather than following the trail all the way around, that could take another hour, and I already can't feel my toes. Mark is standing at the barn with

Andi when we come around the corner. "Hey guys! How did you do? You bunch of slackers. When was the last time you sat on a horse, Jen?"

"Too long ago. I may not be able to walk tomorrow, and I don't want to talk about it." I laugh as I ease Daisy to a stop and place the reins on the horn. "Andi, your girl here is a dream. You're so lucky to have her taking you all over this farm." Andi beams up at me and reaches to Daisy's nose and gives her a scratch. I take the chance to attempt to dismount while Mark is watching her.

"Ha! That was cute Jenna." He remarks from behind me. Darn, he saw. If it looked as bad as it felt, he can laugh all he wants; it's likely warranted. I squat down to stretch my legs and hips and say, "Yeah, yeah, have your fun. I'll get you back."

I smack him on the back of the head just before he ducks out of the way. He's laughing and trying to get away as a ball of snow smacks him perfectly centre on his chest. He looks down at it in fake outrage. I peek out past Daisy's head and see Andi standing there with the biggest grin on her face and remnants of snow on her mittens. She shouts at Mark, "Don't make fun of my Auntie Jenna!"

Mark lunges for her, yelling, "Oh no! You did not just take her side over your own father. Did you see her dismount? You're four feet tall and can do ten times better."

"I don't care. She tried her best, and you're a mean brother." Andi runs full speed away from her dad while he stops to gather snow into a ball. Laughing at the two children having a snowball fight, Liam and I lead the horses back inside the barn to untack and return them to their stalls. The smile on his face, as he watches them over his shoulder makes me stutter in my steps. Pure, unadulterated joy.

He takes Daisy into her stall for me after I've brushed her down while I carry the saddle and bridle back to the tack room. I stand for a moment after I put everything back where it belongs and just absorb the smell of this room. There is nothing like the scent of leather and horse mixed with hay, and it's all made stronger by the cold air coming in from outside. I inhale deeply and close my eyes. This place feels so much like home, just so...right. It makes me think I want to start riding again. I can make a habit of going out with Mark and Andi on their trail rides, or Sara and I can go together. There are so many opportunities, and I don't want to miss them anymore.

Arms wrapping around my waist don't startle me because Liam's arms around me right now is the only thing that can make this moment feel any more perfect than it already did. I turn to whisper into his ear as he rests his head on my shoulder. "This day was perfect." He kisses my cheek and then down my jaw and back to my neck. "Every day with you is perfect, my Jenny girl." I spin around in his arms. "You know how much I love you, right?"

"Yeah, babe, I do, and if it's half as much as I love you, then I'm the luckiest man alive."

I wrap my arms around the back of his head. "I saw you watching Andi and Mark before.... The look on your face... I don't know..." I let my voice trail off because I don't know what I want to ask. I want to know what he was thinking, but I don't want to be the one to bring it up if he wasn't thinking the same thing I was.

"Yeah?"

"What were you thinking about?" He smiles his crooked smile like he's thinking about messing with me, but then his face turns serious, and he leans in and kisses my lips. When he pulls back, his eyes have the super bright shine they get sometimes. "I was thinking that I want that one day. I want to have snowball fights with a little girl that looks just like you."

I can't stop the flood of emotion that swells in my chest, "She has your eyes, though, right?"

"Sure, if that's what you want. And your hair."

"But your teeth, I had braces."

He laughs against my lips. "Sure thing, hun." He peppers kisses down my neck until he reaches my collarbone. Shivers run through my whole body even though I'm still wearing the sweater I layered under my coat for our ride. He spins me around so that the wall is at my back, then walks me backward as his lips press into mine. His tongue finds mine easily, and I get lost in everything that is Liam. His strong arms around me, his fingers in my hair, his masculine scent that screams outdoors and hard work, and his warm mouth on mine. The heat coming off him would melt all the snow on the farm if we were outside, and it's definitely contagious because I could lose some more of these layers now. I can feel every inch of his solid body against mine, and I've never wished to be alone in this barn as much as I do right now—

"Uncle Liam, can you stop kissing Auntie Jenna for a minute to help me throw snowballs at my Daddy?" I break our kiss with a burst of laughter. No charm from me today. Oh well. What you see is what you get with me, I never claimed to be smooth. This kid, though, sure knows how to kill the mood. Liam chuckles as he adjusts himself and spins around to look at our niece. "Sure thing, short stuff, Auntie Jenna can wait for her kisses anyway; can't you, Auntie Jenna?"

Oh, the cheeky bastard. I pull my sweater back down and smile big at him. "I sure can!" Then turning toward Andi, "Let's go get Daddy with those snowballs!"

Andi and I fly out of the barn as fast as we can and start gathering balls of snow. Before we even have enough to start fighting the war they've declared I feel cold, wet snow smack the side of my neck and run down the inside of my shirt. I squeal as I spin around to see Liam standing at the entrance to the barn with a big, goofy grin. Oh, he did not!

"You're going to pay for that, you know?"

His smile only widens, "If you can catch me!" He takes off at a run around the side of the barn while Andi starts hurling balls at Mark. He whips them back just as hard, but each one purposely misses her by a mile. I'm not into high-speed chases through the snow, I make my way slowly and quietly around the other side of the barn with an armful of snowballs. I can catch him off guard and pummel him right in the face.

Just as I'm about to peek around the back corner, knowing I'll see him hiding behind the other, his strong arms wrap around my waist and pull me back into him.

I kick my legs and try to hold onto my weapons, "Argh! Where did you come from? You went the other way!"

He laughs quietly into my ear, "Oh babe, I'm always right behind you." He turns me around and presses my back into the barn wall.

Leaning in against my mouth he says, "Drop your weapons."

Laughter bubbles out of me at his serious tone, but I drop my armful of snowballs in favour of wrapping my arms around his neck. Pulling myself closer to him it's my turn to whisper against his lips, "I love you Liam Ryan."

Turns out I didn't have to wait too long for my kisses. He could melt the snow all around us with this searing kiss. My stomach flutters and my cheeks burn, and I know, without a doubt, that I am exactly where I'm supposed to be.

CHAPTER

Twenty-One

Jenna

The lost days between Christmas and New Years are almost over. It's New Year's Eve, and we are all meeting at the farm for a fire by the pond, along with some skating and drinks until we break off to our own celebrations. I wish Sara and Noah had someone to share these special days with. Noah seems happy in his bachelor status, but Sara seems lonely. I didn't notice it before but the more I pay attention, she does spend a lot of time serving everyone else. She rarely takes time for herself, and I think the right man could make her do that. Someone who loves her and puts her first might show her that she can put herself first, too.

Liam and I pull up to the pond in his truck. There's so much snow you could never get back here without a four-wheel drive, and it's still coming down pretty heavy, but it's not super cold, so it's perfect skating weather. Mark and Sherri are already here. Mark's got the fire going, and Sherri is bundled in her chair with a thermos pressed between her hands.

"Whatchya got in there? Something yummy?" I ask her, pointing at her thermos.

"Oh, you know it! Grab a cup; I'll pour you some."

"Andi, all settled up at the house with mom and dad?" Liam asks Mark.

"Yup, she had two movies picked out and was working on her pillow fort when we headed down here." He shakes his head and laughs. "Crazy girl, but God, I love her."

"We all do, buddy; she's going to be alright; you know?" Liam smacks his back hard enough I'd probably go flying, but Mark just glances at him with an understanding affection. "I know, man. I think we all are."

Sherri and I watch them with soft smiles on our faces. It feels so good to feel the healing that has taken place. We've all come so far, and it doesn't always feel like we have, but moments like this are so precious I want to remember them forever. Noah and Sara pull up in Noah's truck. Sara climbs out with a crockpot of chilli and paper bowls and spoons. Sherri and I jump up to help her. Noah stomps over with skates in hand and hollers. "Who's ready to scrimmage?"

Nothing screams growing up in Ontario like a good old-fashioned game of pond hockey. We all lace up our skates and head out onto the ice. The boys and Sara plow around like professionals while Sherri and I are super wobbly. We probably look like newborn foals trying to stand for the first time. "Come on, Jen, you don't ride anymore, you don't skate anymore either?" Mark yells to me from across the pond.

"Oh, shut up! I don't hear you cutting up your girlfriend; she's sucking too." I look at her apologetically. I can't help but be goaded into arguments with him.

Sherri calls out, "Hey, I'm tryin' here! I didn't grow up skating like you lot." I'll give her that. I am just well and truly out of practice. I was never as big into skating and hockey as the rest of them were, and it shows.

"Hey, Sherri, what do you say we share that beverage you got over there and let these show-offs do their thing?" Sherri laughs but grabs my arm and drags me over to the bench on the edge of the ice. "Sounds like a damn good idea to me."

We unlace our skates and settle in our chairs to watch them skate in circles. They're hooting and hollering, shoulder-checking each other and taking shots at each other, just having the best time. It's so reminiscent of our youth that it almost makes me tear up. But I refuse to get emotional again. I feel like I've done more crying since my dad crashed Christmas dinner than I have all year combined.

"It's so hard for me to imagine what my life would be like if I had stayed in Toronto." I'm thinking out loud, but as usual, Sherri is all ears willing to listen.

"What would it be like? For example, what would you be doing tonight if you'd never moved home?" she asks.

"Well, for starters, I wouldn't be outside. That was one thing I missed so much: there's no nature in the city. I mean, sure, you can seek out a park, but it's not the same. To go skating on New Year's Eve in Toronto means taking public transit to a big rink downtown, surrounded by concrete. It's nice, I guess, if that's all you know. It gets people outside, at least, but this is what I've always had, so this is what I yearned for the whole time I was there."

She nods in understanding. "I get that, so you wouldn't be skating because it couldn't be like this, so what would you be doing? Out at a bar? A party?"

I think about it for a minute. "The New Year's Eve's that I was in university were always spent at house parties. In my first year at my job, I went to a bar with a bunch of girls from work because I wanted to fit in, so I did what they all did, even though I've never been a bar kinda girl. The desire to fit in motivated me, so I had fun, I guess, but it never felt quite right because I wasn't being myself. Last year, I just stayed home. I had already lost that motivation. The truth is, I didn't fit in at work. I was well-liked, but because marketing wasn't my end game, I was never on the same level as everyone else. I didn't see the value in the products we were marketing. I don't believe in the disposable society the entire firm encouraged. I think that was when I became very aware that I needed to start thinking about my exit strategy. Originally, I didn't really have a plan for how long I thought I'd stay and work in the city; I just wanted to gain some experience and boost my confidence. I was no doubt capable of the work and I gave it my all, but that showed me that I can apply the same determination to something that means something to me."

"And that's what you did. You've done it. You're doing it every day. My God, Jenna, you are an inspiration."

I shake my head. "I don't know about that, but I am so happy here, and I am very proud of everything I've accomplished. I don't think I've done anything special. I mean, I have worked hard, but I think a lot of it is also luck and circumstance. I had this amazing town and support system to turn to, to fall back on. I had my mom offering me a place to stay, I have so many opportunities that so many people don't. I think sometimes I can get caught up in all the bad things that have happened to me in my life, and I forget about the blessings."

"You're right, Jen. You are blessed but don't undermine the hard work you've put into your shop, your relationship with Liam, and your savings account before moving home to make it all possible. You earned this success."

I pat her leg in appreciation. "Oh, I know, that is all true. I don't mean to minimize it, and I don't say this just to be super humble. I genuinely want to try to see past the darkness and into the light because there is still so much light in this life we are living."

"You're so right, Jenna. Cheers to that." She reaches out with her thermos and clunks against my cup. We both dissolve into laughter. "Aren't we just a couple of philosophical drunks over here?" Noah drawls as he sits down beside us.

"Just keepin' it real, Noah! What are you up to tonight, after here?" Sherri asks.

As I admitted to staying home last year, I realize I also can't imagine doing anything else after we leave here this year. I promise I'm only twenty-four.

"What time is it? You're going out after here?" I ask incredulously.

"Holy shit Jen, it's only eleven, what are you seventy?" He steals my hat and messes up my hair as he takes a swig of his beer. I think men can only multitask well when they're tormenting.

"I'm making it to midnight, then my ass will be in bed, snuggled in warm, and I'm not ashamed to say it." Sherri bursts out laughing as Mark, Sara, and Liam make their way over to us.

"What's so funny?" Sara asks as she warms her hands over the fire. Noah lifts his camera, which I didn't notice he had and snaps her photo. He answers before I can, "Just making fun of Jenna, being an old lady and wanting to go to bed."

Liam smiles a wicked little smile with a gleam in his eye, then claps his hands together loudly and says, "Sweet, see you guys later. Gotta get my girl to bed."

Mark punches him in the arm without missing a beat. "Argh! Man! That's never not going to be gross. Please. Just don't." We all burst out laughing at Mark's expense, poor big brother.

"I'm heading over to Jerry's after here," Noah finally says when we can stop laughing long enough to hear him. "I'll drive my truck back to my place from here if you guys can give me a ride to his place when you head into town."

Mark agrees. "Sounds good, want to meet me at Sherri's in the morning to head back out here then?"

"Ya, that sounds good. We can swing by home to get cleaned up before lunch?" Mark nods, "Yeah, your mom won't be happy if you show up in day-old clothes with a hangover written all over your face." We all laugh, and Noah shakes his head. "I'm so glad mom said lunch this year. Breakfast on New Year's Day was a bitch to get my ass to." He runs his hands through his hair like he's actually distressed over this.

Liam shakes his head. "Oh Noah, always so hard done by! You can thank Andi for your beauty sleep. Mom and Dad wanted to hog her for the morning, so they pushed us back to noon to give them more time for fun grandparent stuff."

Noah pumps his fist in the air. "Andi, for the win again!"

Mark says, "We'll head out right after midnight. Sherri has a family thing in Scotsville tomorrow. I'm gonna stay the night there. You're planning to leave early to beat the weather comin' in, aren't ya, babe?"

Sherri smiles sadly. "Yeah, even the weather isn't a good enough excuse for my mom. New Year's is her thing, so I have to be there. I missed Christmas, so I can't bail on this."

"Aw, we'll miss you! But we'll plan something together one day next week!"

Mark looks at Sara. "Do you need a ride home? If Noah's coming with us, we can drop you off at your place too."

"Sure, that'd be great, thanks guys."

One of my favourite things about this crew is the comfortable way we chat about anything and everything, but also the comfortable silence. We just sit like this around the fire, feeling the heat, feeling so content, but I know I'm not the only one thinking about Amy. There will always be someone missing from our crew, and that will never change, but on nights like this, it feels like she's here with us. Then, like he's reading my mind, Noah says, "She would fucking love this."

I smile. "She would."

Liam grabs my hand. "She does. She's here with us every day, I think. But I know she's with us right now. She's here for it."

Mark wraps his arm around Sherri. "I wish you could have met her, Sher, she would've loved you."

"I wish that too," Sherri whispers.

I know she used to feel a little weird about being with the whole family and talking about Amy, but everyone's just so happy to see Mark happy that it quickly became a non-issue. Sara's sitting across the fire from me. I see her shoulders shaking just slightly. I can tell she's crying but trying to keep it together. God, my heart breaks for her. I go to her, and from the seat beside her, I can lean in and wrap my arm around her shoulders. "I miss her so fucking much, guys." She sobs, then takes a breath and wipes her tears. "So much it physically hurts. How can it still hurt this bad?"

Mark kneels down in front of her in the snow. "It just does, Sar, because she was that great! When your love is big, so is your loss, and it fucking sucks. She was more than she ever knew, and she left a big fucking hole. I know it hurts, Sara." He wraps his arms around her. "She's seeing you get up every day and living your life, and she's loving that for you. We are hurting, but she isn't. It helps me to remember that if it will help you, take it. We have to use anything we can that helps us get through these days and this life. We only have one life to live, and we can't waste it being sad. No matter how hard it is to smile, we have to look for the light in the darkness because otherwise, what was it all for? I don't want her death to be for nothing. I want it to have changed me for the better. Since losing her, I have loved, I have lived, and I am happy. And I am still sad, but I don't feel guilty for the good times, not anymore. Now I know that I can be both. I will always be sad; it will always be there, just under the surface, but I can't let it control me. I hope you can see what I mean one day, Sara, and I hope you can find the light and then live there. You deserve that. Amy deserves that."

Sara pulls away from his hug and sees her brothers standing in front of her chair. She stands up, and Noah and Liam wrap her in a hug. No one understands exactly what the other feels or is going through, but we can all understand that it hurts. When they break apart, I pour everyone a shot, and we all toast over the fire, "To Amy. To living. One life to live."

It's just after midnight when we shoot those back. Noah is always the comic relief. He grabs his skates and throws them in his truck while yelling back at us, "Thanks for the drinks, suckers!"

Sara hops in Mark's truck, and they follow Noah through the field to the lane. Liam and I are left standing, staring at the fire.

He breaks the silence. "That was pretty intense shit Mark had to say."

"It was, but he's not wrong."

"I know. It's just not as easy as he makes it sound."

"He knows that. He's living it too, Liam, but it's not a race. Maybe you'll never feel the peace and purpose that he does, or maybe you will eventually, but we have to allow our hearts to do what is best for us. Don't get caught up in advice, no matter how good it may be."

He shakes his head. "No, I know, it's not that. Well, maybe it is a little, but it's more that I really do agree with him. I think having you back in my life showed me everything he was saying, but I've been worrying about what that means for my grief and for Amy. Is it okay to be this happy without her here?"

He rubs his hands over his face, and I take one to hold in my hand. "Yeah, it is. I know it can feel wrong, but Mark's right. Live in the light. That's what we're doing. Amy was not darkness. She was everything bright and joyful. I don't want to take that away from her legacy."

I can see his cheeks glisten in the moonlight. "I love you so much, Jenna; you are everything to me." I smile as he takes my other hand. "Now let me take you home."

CHAPTER

Twenty-Two

Liam

After we got home from the farm, we were both so emotionally exhausted we just fell into bed and held each other. We always talk about Amy a lot, but not like that, with all of us together. It's harder, but it feels so good after like we have this one huge thing in common that will always connect us. I think it's good for us to remember that we aren't alone. Our grief is our own, but we can share it with those we love and who loved her and find some understanding there. A little compassion can go a long way to heal a broken heart.

I'm holding Jenna against me, her cheek resting on my bare chest, her breaths long and deep because she's relaxed. I stroke her hair that's falling over my arm that's wrapped around her. She is such a gift. I can't imagine trying to navigate through this without her. There is no way I could have gone on the way I was living with so much resentment and negativity. I make a promise to myself to be here for her when she needs me to lean on like she's been for me. I will spend my life showing her how special and how loved she is. I glance over to my bedside table. I can't see what's in the drawer from here, but I know it's there. A little black box with a ring inside, five small diamonds in the shape of a flower with a sixth in the centre, set on a thin gold band. I can't wait to see it on her finger. I couldn't decide if I was going to wait until after New Year's to ask her to be my wife, but after tonight, I know I can't wait another day. Tomorrow, before we go for lunch at the farm, when we're here alone, having breakfast together, I will beg her to let me love her forever.

I tilt my head down to kiss her head, but she twists back and meets my mouth at just the right moment. My hands find themselves looking for more of her while her hands run up my chest as she moans into my mouth. There is nothing like the feeling of this woman in my bed, with her body next to mine. I vow to myself to cherish her always and to always show her just how much she means to me.

Jenna

"Jenna, come check out the snow coming down!" Liam calls from the living room. I grab our coffees and head in there. "Holy shit, was it calling for all this? It's like a winter wonderland out there?"

"No, it did call for ten centimetres, but we've already got at least twenty, and it's still coming down like crazy. We'll have to take the snowmobile to the main house, there's no way the road will be cleared."

"I wonder how the guys'll get home from town. Sherri doesn't have a snowmobile, but maybe they can just take it slow in Mark's truck. Or wait it out and meet us for supper. Hey, I wonder if Sherri even went to her mother's, depending on when she planned to leave... She could've got ahead of it, I guess."

Liam nods and pats the couch beside him. "I'm sure they'll figure it out. We have an hour before we should head over. Come sit." I smile and ease down onto the couch. Just as I pass him his coffee, I hear my phone ring from the kitchen. "Ugh, I must have left it on the counter." I move to set my coffee on the table, but as my phone quiets, Liam's starts ringing in his pocket. My stomach drops. The hair on the back of my neck stands up as cold runs down my spine.

Something's wrong. I can feel it. I don't know what this feeling is, though.

No, it's fine. I'm paranoid. It's probably nothing.

Liam is talking to somebody; my ears are ringing, and I can't even hear what he's saying.

Focus Jenna. Why does my brain always go to worst-case scenarios? Nothing happened. Everyone is fine. Everything will be okay. It always is.

Except... Not always.

"Jenna."

No.

"It's Mark."

No. No. No. Nooooo!

"Don't. Don't say it."

"Babe... I'm so sorry."

"NO! You aren't sorry. Nothing happened. There's nothing to be sorry for." Liam wraps his arms around me as I sink to the floor. I can hear myself screaming, but it doesn't feel like it's me. I can feel Liam's arms around me, but I can't feel any comfort from them.

I can't feel my own limbs. It's someone else clawing to get away from the man who loves her. It's someone else's life falling apart before my eyes.

I can't breathe. Shit, not now. Not this.

Liam counts, "Breathe in Jen... 1... 2... 3... 4... Now breathe out. 1... 2... 3... 4..."

I try to breathe with Liam's counting, but I can't focus on anything he's saying. All I hear on repeat in my head is, *Jenna, it's Mark. Babe, I'm so sorry.*

This isn't happening.

Mark is fine. He's fine. We're fine.

I saw him ten hours ago. It's okay.

Why did I jump to conclusions again?

I take a deep breath; it fills my lungs. I lift my head from where it's buried in my hands on the floor. I was curled up in a ball with my legs folded beneath me. Liam is rubbing my back, trying to soothe me. I look into his eyes with tears and hope in mine. I overreacted. He's fine, we'll be okay.

What I see in his blue eyes is...utter devastation. I can see his heart breaking all over again. I see the darkness leaching in.

I wasn't wrong.

"Liam, what happened to Mark?" My voice is raw and barely loud enough to hear, but he does hear me. I can tell he does by the flinch I see pass across his face, by the muscle in his jaw that is flexing. I know he heard me because his eyes fill with tears, and they run down his face.

Fuck me, why is this happening to us?

WHY? God, please! Not Mark. Anybody but Mark.

"Liam! What happened? Where is my brother?" He pulls me close to his chest and holds me so tight that it almost hurts, except it doesn't. It feels good to feel something other than this sharp, stabbing tightness in my chest.

"He's gone," he whispers into my hair. I can feel Liam shaking, or maybe I'm shaking. I can't stand, but I can't move. I can't speak or breathe or think.

Mark is gone. My Mark. My big brother.

How? Why?

"Tell me what happened." Liam takes a deep breath, and his trembling hands find mine. We sit back down on the couch, but he doesn't let me go.

"His truck went off the road." His voice cracks with unfiltered grief, and he pauses to get control, "He was just on the edge of town, headed this way, they think—" he drops his head into his hands and lets out a loud sob. "Fuck Jenna, I don't know, I can't do this. How is this happening right now?"

Tears are running down my face. I feel the pain that he is feeling, but

I can't bring myself to comfort him. I feel dead inside. It feels like silence. I don't even know what that means, but it went from chaos to silence. My soul is just.... silent.

I'm staring out the window now, the huge expanse of fields covered in several feet of snow, so clean and pure, such a contrast to how dark and tainted my life feels now. How will I go on without my brother?

My voice is soft despite how harsh it feels. "Who called you?"

"It was Noah." He pauses for a long time, then says, "He said Mark hit a tree head-on. They think there was black ice under the snow. The truck spun completely around and careened into the tree. Everyone's at the farm; they want us to come there if we can. He's gone to get your mom; they'll meet us there."

The farm. My mom. Oh my God, my poor mom. And Andria.... God, Andria! Why is this happening to her?!

"FUCK!!" I scream and punch the couch as I fall over into the cushions. "WHY? WHY HIIM?" Liam reaches for me, but I smack his hand away. "Don't touch me! Not right now. I just can't."

"Jenna, I'm so sorry. I wish I could make this go away."

"Don't say you're sorry! Don't say anything! Just leave me alone!" I'm yelling at him now, and I don't even know why. He didn't do anything. He didn't cause this. He's gotta be dying inside, too. But he's here, and I'm so angry. It feels like rage is boiling inside of me and needs to get out; the only way to release it is to lash out at him.

I burst into tears. I grab his hand in mine. "I'm sorry, Liam. God, I didn't mean that. I don't know what I'm saying or doing."

"Don't be sorry, babe, I'm here, I'll be your punching bag, I'm not leaving. Not now, and not ever. Tell me anything else that you need, and I'll do it, but not that."

"I need to go. We have to go to the farm. I want my mom. And I need to see Andi."

CHAPTER

Twenty-Three

Jenna

We pull up to the house at the farm, and I'm off the snowmobile before Liam's even stopped. Sara runs out the front door; her hair is blowing every which way in the wind, she has no coat, her eyes are bloodshot, and her cheeks are still wet. She opens her arms, and I run into them.

"Jenna. Jenna, God, I'm so sorry. Fuck, I can't even. I can't believe it. What do we do now?" She's crying uncontrollably, and I can't tell her sobs from my own. I pull back slightly. "Where's Andi?"

"She's inside with mom and dad. She's a mess, but she's safe; you don't have to go to her right now. Take a minute, Jen."

"No, I need to see her. I need to hold her. She needs us right now; we should be in there."

Sara rubs both of my arms with her hands and says, "Okay you're right. She's in the living room. Come in, and we'll get warm."

I follow her inside, but I feel like I'm on autopilot. My hat and gloves and boots and snow gear are all in a heap on the floor, but I don't know how they got there. Liam is beside me. I can feel his hand on the small of my back; he's guiding me to the living room.

How is it that last week we sat here and opened gifts together? Mark surprised me with the drama of my dad returning and then we had the best Christmas we've ever had. And now he's gone? Mark no longer walks this earth, and I don't know what to do with that.

Then I see her, my sweet niece. She's curled up on the couch, tucked up into Mrs. Ryan's side, under her arm, protected. Except she isn't. Nothing can protect her from this. Her cheeks are streaked with dried tears, and her lip quivers when she looks up at me. I run to her, and she sits up to fall into my arms on the floor in front of the couch.

"My sweet girl," I mumble into her hair.

"Grandma said that Daddy was in a bad accident. Was he Auntie Jenna? Is Daddy gone away forever?"

I look to Mr. and Mrs. Ryan, then to Sara and Liam. I lay my head on Andria's soft blond hair, and my heart breaks into more pieces than I ever thought possible as I say, "Yes, baby girl, Daddy's gone to Heaven, but just like your Mommy, he will always be here with you. Now they're both watching over you."

My body starts shaking uncontrollably. I can't hold back the sobs that want to escape my throat. "Sit with Grandma, sweetie; Auntie Jenna will be right back." I place her back on the couch and run from the room. I can't fall apart now, not when she needs me more than ever. And my mom needs me. Once out in the hallway, I turn around. "Liam, where's my mom?"

"She's upstairs, laying down. She told Noah she wanted to be alone, but I think you should go up." I head up the stairs and knock on the door that used to be Amy's. "Hey, Mom...." And this is what breaks me; my mom is curled up on Amy's old bed, holding one of Andi's stuffed bears... *Fuck....* It's the one that used to be Mark's; she's rocking back and forth with tears soaking the pillow beneath her face.

"Mom!" I go to her and sit on the edge of the bed. I can't control my tears or my voice. "Mama." I lean my body down so that I'm covering hers, and I brush her hair out of her face.

"How can this be, Jenna? How can he be gone?"

"I don't know, Mom, I really don't know," I choke on a sob as it rises out of my throat. I don't know how to do this. We supported each other when Amy died, but we had to be strong for Mark. We wanted to help him with the baby and make sure he knew he wasn't alone. But now that he's gone, who are we staying strong for? I can feel us breaking. I can feel everything falling apart. I have nothing left to give to anyone, not even my mom.

I hold her tightly and just let it all out; I'm crying and screaming and sobbing. "It hurts so bad, Mom, it hurts. I want him back. I want to say goodbye, I want one more hug, I want to tell him I love him. Mom... I don't know how to get through this life without him."

My mom sits up and wraps her arms around me so that now she's holding me more than I am her. She rubs my back and tells me it'll be okay.

"But will it? How can it be? Nothing will ever be okay ever again."

"Oh, my darling, it will. We will get through this; it's too hard to imagine that now, but I want you to know it and hold on to it for dear life. We aren't okay right now, but we will be."

CHAPTER

Twenty-Four

Jenna

I can't stop crying. No matter how hard I try. I didn't know it was humanly possible to cry for days. Now I know it is. But I wish I still didn't know. We are all at the farm again today. I don't know why or how it became our meeting house. I think just because no one wants to go to Mark's for anything other than necessities for Andi, my mom's is too small for us to fit comfortably, so we just always end up here. My mom's been spending a lot of time at home with my dad; him being here has turned out to be more of a blessing than we ever could have imagined.

Noah drove to Scotsville to get Sherri; no one wanted her driving that far in such an emotional state and with the weather being so unpredictable. So, she's been here with us most days, but she hasn't said much. She seems torn between being lost in her own grief and trying to comfort the rest of us. Typical Sherri, always caring for everyone else. There is no right answer to how to handle any of this, though; we're all just doing what we can to get through each day.

Sara is off work for the foreseeable future and has been staying here at the farm to take care of Andi. Liam has enough seasoned staff at his store to leave it to sort of run itself, and I've closed the shop until further notice.

It feels like life has been put on hold, but at the same time, it keeps moving forward. Somehow, I'm getting out of bed every day; I'm going to meetings at the funeral home with my mom, and I'm spending my days here with Andi and everyone else. Liam hasn't left my side, and I can't decide if I'm grateful for that or if I want him to go away. I hate seeing him hurting; it feels like when Amy died all over again, except I can't even think straight to worry about what he might be needing from me right now. I am doing all the things that constitute living, but it doesn't feel like I can do it another second longer without Mark. Every day, I think I can't do this again today, but then I do. Somehow.

I'm standing at the front of the chapel at the funeral home while Liam speaks about my brother. He's telling everyone what an amazing guy he was, the best friend, brother and dad to us all; he's crying and laughing through memories while I stand beside him, trying to control my shaking hands.

I can't stand the past tense. I want to scream at him to shut up and stop saying 'was,' but I know I can't, and he can't, so I keep quiet; I stare at the floor to avoid eye contact with everyone out there who's looking at me, pitying me.

How did I become someone who's lost their sibling? How am I an only child now? I don't know how to be an only child. How the fuck can anything ever be as it should be ever again?

Noah is sitting in the front row beside Sherri, with Andi on his lap. She looks so small wrapped in his arms, but her eyes are wise beyond her years. In almost seven years, that girl has experienced more heartache than anyone should ever have to in an entire lifetime, but she sits there quietly with her eyes on her Uncle Liam. She has tears in her eyes, but she smiles when everyone laughs at a memory Liam is recalling. My sweet girl will never have the joy of growing up with Mark tucking her into bed at night, embarrassing her at school drop-off, or making fun of her clothes in high school. He'll never take her photo before prom; he won't be there to walk her down the aisle at her wedding. He will never get to be a grandpa to her babies one day. She will miss out on getting to experience all of those things with him by her side.

Then I realize, he won't be at my wedding either; I always thought he would walk me down the aisle. That feels like a punch to my stomach, and I almost double over as I think of everything I will miss out on with him. I glance over to my mom and dad sitting beside Liam's parents. My dad holds my mom while she cries into his shoulder. The Ryans look similar. Mark was so loved and will be missed by so many.

I never thought I would be so grateful for my dad's presence, but I can see how much my mom needs him now, and he's here, being there for her. He must be completely broken inside, but you wouldn't know it, not the way he's holding her up every day, strong and steady at her side. He's never been that person for her, but if this is the only time in his life that he can do it, then I will be eternally grateful.

Liam has stopped speaking and takes my hand in his. He looks at me, silently asking if I want to say anything. I shake my head, and he leads me back to our seats between Noah and Sara. The rest of the service goes by in a blur; there are songs played that I chose with my mom, and there's a prayer spoken that made my mom feel some peace about what waits for us after we leave this earth. None of it matters to me, though; I can't make myself care or feel anything but pain. My body physically hurts; I can't sleep, but I can't stand to be awake knowing he's no longer here. Everything I eat tastes like ash in my mouth; I keep eating anyway because Liam suggested my mom was starting to worry about me, and I don't want to add to her burden.

Everyone's milling about now, eating and drinking while they mourn and celebrate who Mark was. I haven't left my mom's side, but she pats me on the shoulder now and says, "Jenna, dear, go home. You look exhausted, and you don't need to be here any longer."

"Mom, I don't want to leave you, I'm fine."

"Oh, your father's here; he's been a Godsend, I'll be alright a little while longer, and then he'll bring me home. He's been staying in the spare room, so I'm not alone. You go to Liam's and spend some time with him; he needs you right now as much as you need him, you know?" I wince at the thought of sitting alone with Liam and my grief, *our* grief. It feels like too much to know he's hurting so much, too, but I can't help him. I'm drowning in my own grief, and it's leaving me with nothing left to give him.

"I think I'll just go home to your house; I'll lie down for a while. Wake me when you get back, though, okay?"

She looks at me with a mix of disapproval and understanding and says, "Okay, hun, if that's what you want."

"It is."

I find my coat and make my way to the door when I feel Liam's hand wrap around my wrist. No one's touch feels quite like his, like a spark shooting from my fingertips right to my heart. I feel a slight smile on the inside at the thought that he's still my Liam, even in the dark. He's here, loving me, and when it feels like everything is lost, that never will be, but the smile never makes it to my face. I can't even think about anything that might make me happy or feel good without thinking that Mark will never feel anything ever again.

"Jenna, where are you going?" Liam has a crease between his eyebrows as he looks into my eyes.

"I just need to get out of here. I'm gonna go home and lie down."

He reaches for his keys. "Okay... okay no problem, yeah, we can go home, that's a good idea." I rest my hand on his arm. "Liam, I'm going to go to my mom's. I just want to be alone for a while." My heart sinks at the look on his face. If there was a way to hurt someone more than we're all already hurting today, then I just did it.

Fuck, I'm an asshole.

But I can't be near him right now. I just need to be away from all the pain. I can't outrun my own, but I can run away from his. He looks at me pleadingly like he can read my mind. "Jenna. Do not shut me out."

"I'm not. Okay maybe I am, but just for right now. I just need this time, Liam, please. You said you'd give me anything I needed."

"I said I would do anything but leave you!" I start to cry again, if I ever even stopped. "Please don't be mad, please. I just have to go."

At that, I turn and walk out the door.

CHAPTER

Twenty-Five

Jenna

It's been two months since Mark's accident. Just as I feared it would, life went on.

I eventually had to open my shop up again. I still feel like I'm just going through the motions to get through each day. I don't feel the same drive to live and love and enjoy everything that I did before he died.

This is grief.

Jamie put that offer in on the house I wanted before he left for the holidays, and it was accepted. They kindly accommodated our time of loss and pushed the closing date to March for me.

Like the blink of an eye, March is here, and I need to start thinking about moving out of my mom's house and into my own.

It doesn't hold the same lustre that it did before Christmas, but she swears she'll be okay. My parents have kinda sorta made their way back to each other in these last couple of months, and it's been pretty cool to see. I know, even at Christmas, there were no hard feelings between them; they had worked through all of that before I even was aware my dad was around. They've leaned on each other so much since Mark died that I think they've found a place in each other's hearts that wasn't there before. Dad moved back into the house a few weeks ago, so at least now I know my mom won't be alone when I move out. The time spent with both of them together has been amazing for my relationship with my dad. I was still holding onto resentment for him leaving, but with Mark gone now, I just want to honour his wishes as best I can, and he wanted me to get to know who my dad is now. He wasn't wrong, of course. Annoying even when he's not here.

But seriously, I am learning that my dad is a great guy. He made some poor choices and hurt a lot of people, but he's making amends every day by sticking around.

I'm heading to Liam's Coffee and Books to meet Liam for lunch, and then we're going to go over to the new house to check everything over one more time before I get the keys on Monday.

He's been my rock these last couple of months. I don't know how he's wading through his own grief along with mine, too, but he's doing it, and I'm so grateful to him.

He's talking with Sherri behind the counter when I walk through the door. They both look up and smile. "Hey there!" Sherri waves and starts making me my favourite coffee.

Liam comes around the counter and wraps me in a hug. "Hey, my Jenny girl, ready to go?"

"Sure, let's go." Sherri passes me my coffee with a smile, and I say, "Thanks, Sher, we'll catch up tomorrow, OK? It's been a while."

"Definitely. You know where to find me." Liam and I walk out the door and head to his truck to make the short drive to my house.

My house.

That sounds so foreign to me, but I think it's a good step for me; I hope it is, anyway.

"Liam, do you think this is still the right thing for me to do?" He stops in front of his truck and looks at me with his eyebrows pinched in confusion. "What do you mean? The house? Sure, it's what you want, right? It's part of your plan."

"I know, yeah, it was the plan. I just don't know anymore. I don't know if the plan matters. Why do I need my own place? If I want out of mom and dad's, I can move in with you; I don't know if any of this is worth it anymore, that's all."

"Let's go have a look at it. Jamie's waiting there for us anyways, and we can see how you feel once we're there, okay?"

"Okay, that sounds good. Thanks for listening to me and not thinking I'm a crazy person." We walk around to each of our doors and get in the truck. As he's sliding in, he laughs. "Oh, I definitely think you're a crazy person, but I love your crazy." He leans across the console of the truck and kisses me gently.

I am so lucky to have this man. I wish I could return the love and devotion he's giving me, but instead, I feel so empty and monotonous. It's not fair to him, but I can't seem to snap out of this heavy overwhelm of sadness.

Jamie is waiting for us, like Liam said. He unlocks the door but stays on the porch to give us a chance to walk through and discuss anything, just the two of us. Liam looks at me hopefully. "Well, is it still everything you remember?"

I laugh lightly. "I guess I don't really know; I just don't care anymore. I don't know how else to say it."

He takes both of my hands in his own and says, "You're sad, Jen. That's allowed, that's normal, or expected, whatever word you want to use, but it can't mean that your life ends. You can't stop caring about yourself; you're too important to too many people to stop living your life. You can drown in your grief, or you can turn it into love. Love for life, love for the people you have left and love for yourself. Love yourself enough to carry on."

He moves his hands to my cheeks and holds my face ever so gently. "This house was everything to you, once. I get that it isn't everything anymore, but it's still something. Your reasons for buying it haven't gone away; they just aren't important right now, and that's okay. I think you should go ahead with the purchase, but if you don't want to move here right now, then don't. Move in with me or move in here, wherever you're going, to feel like your best self. Either way, it will be here, and it will be yours, just like you wanted."

I give him a small, sad smile. "When did you become so wise and understanding?" He pulls me into a hug. "When the love of my life needed me to be."

I decide to do exactly what Liam suggested, we leave with plans to meet Jamie again on Monday to get the keys.

It turned out Sherri had the afternoon off the next day, so we had our coffee in the morning on her break but made plans to meet up again in the afternoon and try to coerce Sara into taking the afternoon off, too.

She blows through my door, sending the bell tinkling like crazy; I look up from the bouquet I'm arranging and, with raised eyebrows, say, "Hey, Sherri, what's the hurry?"

She laughs her big, boisterous laugh and waves her hand at me as if to say, 'Pfft,' but she says, "Oh no hurry, but I'm heading home to my mom's for a bit, so I wanted to get here to spend as much time with you as I can!"

"Oh, that's so nice! I didn't know you were going home to visit again. How long are you staying?"

She winces a little, "That's the thing, I don't know when I'll be back." She waits quietly for my reaction. I can't even explain why, but I burst into tears. I wave my hand quickly in front of my face, saying, "Oh my God, Sherri, I'm so sorry. I don't know what's wrong with me. I'm such an emotional wreck. But you're leaving? Like leaving, leaving?"

"No! Well, yes, sort of. I don't know. I just have to get away, and I'm so sorry if that hurts you. I know you need all the support you can get right now, but I just can't be in this town, just for a little while."

I wipe the tears from my face and nod. "I get that. Boy, do I ever get that! Remember who you're talking to? I'm going to miss you so much, though." I walk out from behind my counter and embrace her with every fibre of love and understanding I can muster. "When do you leave?"

"Tonight. I wanted to spend this afternoon with you and Sara, and then I'm hitting the road."

"Does Liam know?"

"He does now; he didn't before today; I'm sorry I made all these plans so last minute; I didn't mean to screw him over for staffing."

"Oh gosh, I'm sure he can figure it out. He'll just be happy you're doing what you need to do for yourself."

She smiles. "That's exactly what he said. He's one of the good ones, you know?" She has tears welling in her eyes now. "Don't let that one go Jenna." That makes me freeze as I pull back from our hug; she looks at me quizzically. "Jenna? What? What's wrong?"

"He is one of the good ones. He's the best. And I am so broken now. I don't know what I have to offer him anymore." Tears come pouring down my face, and I can't stop the sob that erupts from my throat. I turn away from her because I can't believe I'm saying this out loud. What am I even doing anymore? Sherri interrupts my thoughts by saying, "Jenna! What the fuck? What do you mean?"

"I don't know, Sherri; I just don't know anything anymore. I feel like all he does is give, give, give, and all I can do is take, take, take, and it's not fair. But I can't stop it. I feel like I'm floating through my days with no feeling and no direction, and he's just along for the ride."

She grabs my arms. "Jenna. Don't push him away; don't make the same mistake you did when Amy died. Talk to him this time. Go through it together."

"It's not the same. I can't push past this; I can't just talk my feelings away. It hurts so fucking bad."

"You think he doesn't know that. Do you forget he's been exactly where you are?" Her face is all screwed up, and she's yelling at me now, but I deserve it; I am so fucked up.

"I know, I know!" I rub my face with my hands. "I don't know, I just don't know anything anymore."

Sara comes through the door as I'm wiping tears from my face, and she freezes. "What's wrong? What happened?"

We are all so conditioned to think the worst anymore; I hate the fear in her eyes just because she sees me upset. Thankfully, Sherri goes to her quickly, "Nothing really; I just told Jenna I'm going home to my moms for a while, and she's upset; it's okay, though. I'm not sure how long I'll be gone. I want us to have this afternoon together, and then I'm heading out."

Her eyes widen in shock much like I imagine mine did. "What? Sherri! Are you sure that's what you want?"

She nods her head. "Yes, it's what I need. I know I'll be OK eventually; I know I will be back; I love this town, and I love you guys too much to stay away. I just need a bit of time to let it sink in and heal over a little, you know?" She glances back at me. "Jenna, I can't begin to imagine how you're feeling now, but I think how I'm feeling might be similar to why you left after Amy. It's like your grief is too big for my heart to carry along with my own. And that's not your fault or mine; it can't be helped at all. I think it comes with loving you guys and loving Mark. It was fucking worth it, let me tell you! It still is worth it. But I do need to go, just like you did. I will be okay, though; I have faith in that."

The three of us pile into a group hug and wipe each other's snot and tears all over each other; in a few minutes, we're all laughing and crying, and it feels good. It's been so long since I laughed. I almost forgot what it felt like.

When we pull apart, we look into each other's eyes and burst out laughing again. Anyone looking in would think we'd all lost our minds, and maybe we have. Sara grabs my arm, and I take Sherri's hand. "Who wants pizza?"

They both say, "Me!" at the same time, and we laugh and head out the door. We make our way to Sara's apartment to watch Friends and eat pizza before we say goodbye to another friend, but not forever this time, just for now. For now, I can put my worries about Liam aside and enjoy my last afternoon with my best friends.

CHAPTER

Twenty-Six

Jenna

I moved into my house yesterday.

I do love it. I thought I wouldn't. I said I didn't care but sitting on the porch right now, reading my book, sipping my tea, watching the rain come down, is bringing something out in me that I thought was gone. A sense of calm and peace that I thought died with Mark. It's the first time I've felt anything close to content since he died.

It's been almost three months. Sherri's been gone for a couple of weeks, but we talk or text every day. She's doing well and enjoying spending time with her family. She hasn't spent much time with them at all since she settled here in Balsam River. I don't know much about her history; she always said she wanted to leave it behind, but it seems that she's changed her mind about that. Death can do that to a person.

It makes you rethink everything you thought you knew about life. Liam's truck pulls into the driveway, and I smile and wave at him from where I'm sitting on the wicker couch. He lumbers up the steps with a big smile on his face. He's so happy all the time. It's gotta be fake, and I hate it.

I hate that my smile is fake, too. I hate how we've started tiptoeing around each other.

He leans down to kiss me, and I kiss him back, but then his hands travel down; his fingers tease the waistband on my leggings and then slide up under my shirt; I can't stop myself from pulling away. "Liam, don't."

He frowns. Okay, he's always happy until I say that I guess.

"Don't what?" His voice is soft, and I can tell he's hurt by my words, "What's wrong with wanting to kiss you and touch you, Jenna?"

There is no malice in his tone; he's genuinely perplexed and maybe a little worried about me, about us. It's been months. Almost three. Since the night before Mark died.

Every time we almost, it takes me back to that night, how it was the last one he was alive, how happy we were. I hate knowing I will never feel that again. And it feels wrong to let Liam touch me and be even remotely close to feeling that way again.

I try to explain this to him. I don't know if I'm making any sense; I'm rambling, I think. He looks more and more confused the more I talk. I finally stop, take a breath, and look him in the eyes.

"Do you know what I mean? Can you understand how hard it is for me?"

"Of course, my Jenny girl, I had no idea. I thought it was me. I thought I upset you somehow. You have to keep talking to me, Jenna; I want to know everything going on inside your head and your heart."

I smile because he's so fucking wonderful. I don't deserve this man's love. The things Sherri and I talked about the day she left, keep ringing in my head, that he's too good, giving me too much. She thought I was crazy, but I see how hurt he is by me in this moment, and I want to be more for him. But I don't have any more to give. How long will he hold the pieces of me in his hand and keep loving them?

The rest of the month feels like I'm just going through the motions. Liam was right about the house, though. It's been good for me; it's given me something to care for and somewhere to go each day that is all my own. Just like I thought it would be before everything. I lost that along the way, but I'm glad he kept sight of my goals when I couldn't.

I'm having Andi over tonight for the long-awaited sleepover. Sara has been slowly moving into Mark's house, and that's been an adjustment for everyone, but one that we all agreed would be best for Andi. I've wanted to spend more time with her to make sure she's doing OK and to make sure she knows how important and loved she is. I don't want her to ever feel alone in this world, although I know she's bound to at some point in her life, I just want her to know where she can turn to for unconditional love and support when that happens. Giving Sara a break and a chance to get settled is just an added bonus to this night together.

I pick her up from the farm because that's where she spends her afternoons between school letting out and when Sara gets off work. We pick up pizza and pop with a side of popcorn and gummy bears on the way home.

"What movies do you have picked out to watch tonight, Andi?" I ask her as we push through my front door with all our goodies.

She smiles and excitedly says, "I picked my two favourite Christmas movies!" I laugh. What a crazy kid. "Christmas movies? It's April. What's up with that?"

I watch her face fall into a frown, and my heart sinks; what did I say? She's not usually that sensitive to jokes or sarcasm, but maybe she's changed since Mark died. I hate that I don't really know if she has. I couldn't bring myself to spend much one-on-one time with her before now. I was a selfish asshole and protected myself before her. It hurt me too much to see her, so I left her hurting. I know she wasn't alone; she had the whole Ryan family surrounding her, but I am her family, too. I am Mark's family, and I should have been there.

I wrap my arms around her and pull her into my lap as I sit on the couch. "What's wrong, bug? What did I say?"

She shakes her head, but her lip trembles. "Is it weird to watch Christmas movies in April?"

"No, not at all! We can watch any movie any time of year. It's okay, I'm sorry I made you feel like it was weird. I love Christmas movies. Which ones are we watching?"

She smiles tentatively. "The Grinch and Rudolph."

"I love those ones!" I say excitedly. But her smile is more sad than excited. What she says next tells me all I need to know about how much she needs me right now.

"Me too. Rudolph was Daddy's favourite, and The Grinch is mine. Daddy did the best Grinch voice. We watched them both a lot before he left."

I feel like I've been punched in the stomach and had my heart removed and stomped on at the same time. As tears run down my cheeks, I tell her, "Baby, we can watch these movies whenever you want, as many times as you want. If there's anything in this world that helps you remember your daddy, then I want you to hold on tight to it, and you know what? I want to be a part of it if you'll let me. Thank you so much for choosing these movies for me to watch with you. It means so much to me to be able to remember your daddy with you."

"Is it hard not having a brother anymore, Auntie Jenna?"

I swallow hard so that I can answer her without falling apart, "It sure is, baby girl. The hardest thing I've ever had to do. It's not as hard as it is not having your mommy or daddy anymore though. You are so brave, and I'm so proud of you."

"I'm so happy I have you and Aunt Sara to take care of me, and Uncle Liam and Uncle Noah remind me of Daddy. They make me laugh like he did." Her little hands wrap around my neck, and I let myself fall apart a little bit while she rests her head on my shoulder.

We spend the night snuggled into each other on the couch, watching hers and my brother's favourite Christmas movies, just so we can hold on to that last Christmas a little while longer.

The next day, I take Andi to Liam's store and let her choose a book, and we get our favourite sugary drinks and sit and read in the front window for as long as she wants to. It's one of the best weekends I've had in a long time.

Liam joins us for lunch, and even that feels lighter than it has been. Something has shifted just a little bit, and I feel like I can breathe a little easier. I don't know if he notices how distant and solemn our relationship has been; I have been trying to be better to him. I try to tell him how I'm feeling, but I hate being a Debbie downer all the time, so I am still holding back more than I should.

I just think of how heavy all these emotions are to me, and they're my own; I don't want to put them on him, too! More than anything, I just want to be my old self again. I can't seem to ward off this sadness. Sometimes, I wonder what normal grief is and when I should start considering that I may be suffering from depression. I don't know how to tell the difference, but I know that this feels never-ending, and that scares the shit out of me.

I think I'm putting up a good front, but I can only carry this 'fake it till you make it' for so long.

I need something to shake me out of this funk.

I keep thinking, something's gotta give, Mark isn't coming back, and I cannot keep living this half-life. What can I do to get my ass in gear? What will bring me joy right now?

I look around the coffee shop, and the absence of someone's beautiful laugh and smile makes me realize what I need to do.

Yes.

I will go see Sherri.

I know from experience that getting out of this town and away from the memories can help. Maybe I just need a little time away. I can live a different life, not the sad one that pulls on me here, just for a little while until I feel better than I do right now.

I call Jamie and ask him if he can list the house for a tenant, fully furnished, whatever term he can get. I'll take my personal stuff back to Mom's, pack my suitcase, and get out of here. He says he'll list it and call me if he gets any prospects. I'm not going to wait for that, though; it can sit empty until he finds someone. I ask him to meet me at my shop in the morning, and I'll sign whatever needs to be signed before I go.

I look up from the arrangement to see Jamie coming in the door. "Hi Jamie, thanks for doing this on short notice; I'm heading out of town and want to get this squared away before I go."

He frowns. "You're leaving town? I thought you had decided to move in with Liam sooner than planned. But you're leaving?" He rubs his hands down the front of his coat like he's nervous, "Shit, that must have wrecked Liam. Guy's been head over heels for you since we were kids."

Fuck, crap, shit.

Liam. I haven't even told Liam. I can't. He'll try to stop me. I need to do this.

"Umm, I haven't talked to Liam about this. I'm just really struggling lately, Jamie, and I need a change of scenery. I'll be back; I think this will just help to bump me out of this slump I can't get out of. He will understand. I'm going to call him once I get to Sherri's and get settled. It'll be okay, trust me."

Jamie shakes his head. "I don't know you all that well, Jenna, but I know Liam, and this will not be okay. You need to talk to him before you go and explain; if he'll understand later, then he'll understand even better now."

I rub my face with my hands. "I can't Jamie, I can't face him. You're right, and he won't let me leave, but I have to. I can't see the hurt on his face. I can't watch his heart break again. I don't know what else to do. I'm sinking in this grief, and I can't get above it."

"Talk to him. Stay, fight this together. Don't do this again." He pauses because my head turns towards him sharply. "Don't think I don't know that you've already done this to him. It's a small town, Jenna, and Liam's a good guy; he doesn't deserve this."

Ugh, damn small towns. "I know! I just need to get out of here, OK?" I'm yelling now, and I don't even know why.

The doorbell jingles behind me, and I spin around. "Sara."

She shoots daggers at me with her eyes. "Please don't tell me you're leaving my brother, Jenna." I close my eyes and tilt my head back to look at the ceiling. If I open them, they will be filled with regret. This isn't how I planned any of this. Who am I kidding? I didn't even plan any of this at all.

"I just don't think I can stay here. I'm going to Scotsville to see Sherri." Jamie looks at me with so much disappointment in his eyes, but I can't worry about that. This is what I need. Time, space, somewhere new. Not forever, I don't think, just for now.

Sara turns on her heel and walks out of my flower shop without a backward glance. Jamie runs after her, and I'm left alone in my shop, feeling like the one thing I think might save me just might ruin everyone else.

CHAPTER

Twenty-Seven

Liam

Sara storms into my office and slams the door behind her. Her face is flushed red, and her eyes are bloodshot from crying. My heart jumps into my throat. Fuck, what happened now.

Please, no more tragedy, not now and not ever. I can't take anything else terrible happening. I'm hanging on by a thread here and barely hanging on to Jenna. I think she's slipping further and further away from me every day. I stand up from my desk so quickly that my chair flips over backwards; in two strides, I'm standing in front of my sister, "Sara, what is it? What's wrong? Tell me!"

"She's leaving. She's leaving again!" She's shaking now. I don't know if she's angry or sad or what the fuck is going on, and who's leaving?

"Who Sara? Calm down. Who's leaving?" My heart feels like it's being ripped out of my chest because, while I realize who she's talking about, she looks me in the eyes and says, "Jenna!"

"No." That's all I get out, just one word.

No. This can't be happening. She wouldn't do this again. She just bought a fucking house down the street from here.

"Yes. I just saw her an hour ago, and she was talking with Jamie, and she said she's leaving for Sherri's."

"An hour ago? And you're just coming to me now? What the fuck Sara, she could be gone by now!"

I run out onto the street, heading towards Jenna's Blooms, but when I get there, the lights are off, and the door is locked. She can't just leave her business, and her parents, her house. She's not leaving for good. I need to calm the fuck down. I get my phone out of my pocket, go to my favourites, and press on her name. I listen to it ring until her voicemail picks up. "Jenna! Hun, it's me; please call me back. I talked to Sara, so please call me back as soon as you get this and tell me what's going on. Let me know what you need and let me know you're safe. I love you."

I shove my phone back in my pants pocket then yank it back out again and call Sherri. No answer there either. These fucking women always stick together, thank God for sibling loyalty, or I'd still be in the dark. Shit, I left Sara in my office. I make my way back there to check on her and see what else she knows. She's sitting in my chair with her arms resting on my desk and her head on her arms.

"Sara, what else did she say? She must be already on her way there; the shop was closed."

She looks up at me and says, "I don't know, Liam; I didn't even talk to her, really; I was just so angry that she was doing this to you again that I stormed out. I know she's hurting, but it's not fucking fair, we are all hurting, doesn't she know that?"

She's crying now. "I know, Sara, and she knows that too. She's not leaving for good. It's okay, trust me. It'll be okay. You overreacted. She might need some time away, but she has her shop here, and she just bought a house, and thanks for the vote of confidence, but she loves me, you know? She wouldn't just bail on what we have."

I hope my tone lightens her mood a little bit. I want her to understand that this isn't as bad as it seems. Granted, I can't get a hold of Jenna to confirm that, but I know what I know. She isn't running away from me;

she's running away from her broken heart. It may be similar to what she's done in the past, but this time, I know what she's going through, and I know what she's feeling, and I know that she loves me. It couldn't be more different. Because this time...I will not let her go.

Sara stands from where she was sitting at my desk and comes to me with her arms open. "I'm sorry, Liam, you're probably right. That all makes so much sense. I just lost it. I should have stayed and talked to her. I'm so sorry."

"Ssshhh, it's okay, don't worry about it. I'll go find her, and we'll talk it out and see what she needs. I know it'll be okay, Sara. I will not lose another person that I love. Not right now."

Sara heads back to the farm to spend the afternoon with Andi. I told her I'd keep her posted whenever I have an update. My next move is to do whatever I can to get to Jenna. I pick up my phone to text my brother.

Liam: *Hey, where are you?*

Noah: *Just leaving the station. Why? What's up?*

Liam- *I need your help; meet me at your place.*

Noah: *Sure, see you in ten.*

I fill Noah in on what Sara told me. I don't know much else since Jenna or Sherri haven't called me back. "So where do I come in? I don't know the first thing about getting a woman back."

"Fuck you, Noah, I'm not *getting her back*, she didn't leave me. I haven't even talked to her yet, I just—"

"Yeah, that's not a good sign." He smirks. I smack him on the back of the head, "I need you to tell me where Sherri's parents' place is. If Jenna's going to see her, then that's where I'll find her. I'm not letting her just take off without talking to me first."

Rubbing the back of his head, Noah says, "But isn't she already gone?" I raise my hand to hit him again, but he ducks. "Okay, I guess I'm going to get her back then, you asshole."

His shit-eating grin has me shaking my head; it is good to see him smile, even if it is at my expense. I know he's been really struggling these last couple of months.

Fuck, we all have, what can any of us do but plow through this bullshit. It's too much loss for one family to handle. But here we are, handling it the best we can anyway.

"Hey man, why don't you come with me for the drive?"

"Why the fuck would I want to do that?" He laughs, so I know not to take him too seriously.

"Because it'll be good to get out of town for a day or two, and why the fuck not?" He rubs his hand back and forth over his hair; buddy needs a haircut and a shave now that I'm looking, but he smiles and says, "Alright, 'why the fuck not' it is. I'm driving. I don't want to get stranded in the middle of your lover's spat."

"Noah, don't be an asshole to Jenna when we get there, you know she's hurting." He lowers his eyes and then turns his back on me. I know he's protecting himself with his humour, but I need him to be careful around Jenna.

"I know, Liam, I know. I'm sorry, man; I just don't know how to deal with this shit. I didn't know how to seven years ago, and I'm not any better now. If anything, I'm worse at it, but I would never hurt Jenna, you know that. Fuck me, I'd give anything to take this pain away from her. We know what it's like to lose one of us, but what if we were the only ones left? It was just the two of them, and now he's gone. She must feel so alone. Just fuckin' breaks my heart."

He's full of piss and vinegar most of the time, but then he comes out with some of the most insightful shit, and I can't shake how much truth there is in words.

I've felt like this whole time that I knew what Jenna was going through, but I don't really. It's not the same; nothing can ever be the same. Just like Noah's loss of Amy was different from mine. How could I have compared them for even a second?

The drive is just over three hours to get to Sherri's. I wonder if Noah is remembering the last time he had to drive up here. Sometimes, I'm so focused on Jenna that I lose sight of what everyone else around me is going through. I know Sara has her hands full with Andi. She's spent the last couple of weeks officially moving into Mark's house. She thought it would be best for Andi to get to stay in her home, and she's probably right. That doesn't make it any easier on her, though.

Noah lost his best friend and neighbour. His coworker. His brother in every way that matters. Fuck, why can't I remember how much things affect everyone differently? It's so hard to navigate everything and everyone. Some days, I think I might crumble under the pressure to make sure everyone is happy and healthy.

Noah is sitting beside me and looks relatively well put together, but I can hear that he's grinding his teeth, Sara is perpetually on the brink of tears, and Jenna fucking left town without telling me. I think it's fair to say I'm not doing this well.

"I was going to ask Jenna to marry me, you know?" Noah snaps his head to look at me, then turns it quickly back to the road.

"When? Now? That's fucking huge, Liam; why are you bringing me along for that?" I laugh a little too loudly. "Ha! No, on New Year's Day. I had the ring. I looked at it the night before after she fell asleep and made my plan for breakfast, and then we could celebrate with everyone at the lunch at the farm."

I see his knuckles turn white as he clenches the wheel a little tighter, but all he says is a low "Fuck."

I nod. "Yeah. Fuck."

We sit in silence for a long time after that. I don't know why I felt the need to tell him that. It doesn't matter now. Nothing matters if she doesn't fucking come back. I think I just wanted to share a piece of what was with him. There's so much that could've been and now never will be, but that one felt like a secret, and it feels good to have shared it with my brother. He interrupts my thoughts when he says, "You'll ask her another day. She'll say yes. We will be happy again. I promise you, brother."

Tears spill from my eyes at his words.

"Do you believe that Noah, were you even happy before? How long does it take? How long will it take this time? I'm so fucking tired of hurting, of waiting and losing. I'm fucking tired!" I'm yelling at him now, but not *at* him. I'm yelling at this fucking shit life that keeps happening to us instead of letting us just live it.

He doesn't turn to look at me again, but I can see the tears glistening on his cheeks as he says, "I know, Liam. Me too."

We drive the rest of the way in silence.

CHAPTER

Twenty-Eight

Liam

We pull up to Sherri's house and Jenna's waiting on the front porch. I texted her that I was on my way and that if she left before I got there, I would torment Sherri and her parents with my sob story until she came back. I'm happy to see she took my threats seriously. Noah hops out of the truck and heads for the door. She comes down the porch steps, and as she tries to sidestep out of his path, he grabs her and wraps his arms around her. Hard. I can see him whisper something in her ear, and she wipes under her eyes.

She's heading this way again; I hop out of my side and hold the door open for her. She slides in, and I walk around the front to the driver's side. Noah waves from the porch as Sherri opens the front door for him. As I'm backing out of the driveway, I notice him wrapping Sherri in a hug, too. fuckin' guy just found his emotions or what?

I shake my head with a light laugh, and Jenna looks at me funny. I point to Noah and Sherri in the doorway, like she can read my mind, and she laughs to herself, too.

"What did he say to you back there?" I ask her tentatively, unsure if I really want to know.

"Nothing, just gave me a hug."

"I saw you wipe your eyes. What did he say?"

Her voice hardens as she says, "Liam, nothing. Just drop it."

I can take a hint; I'll just ask him later.

"Where are we going?"

"I just thought we could sit at the park around this bend here and talk for a bit. If you want to go back to Sherri's after, I'll take you back. I'm not holding you hostage, Jen. I just want you to hear me out, and I want to know what's going on with you, what all this is about." I wave my hand in the general direction of the outside.

"You're not going to yell and scream at me that I left without talking to you?" I pull into a parking space in the lot I saw on the way into town.

"No, Jenna, it was a crazy thing to do, and I don't understand it, but I don't think I understand much of anything anymore. I said I'll take you back to Sherri's but I'm not going home without you. I'm not going to keep going on like this; I want to understand; I want to know your heart like I used to."

"What? What do you mean? You can't stay here, Liam; I don't even know how long I'm staying."

"I'm not leaving you. We will work out whatever is going on with you together. I have a feeling it has nothing to do with me, and that's fine, but I'm here anyway."

She shakes her head incredulously. "I just needed to get away, a change of pace, change of scenery, call it whatever you want. I'm tired of being sad all the time. I hate it!"

I turn to her and take her hand; I rub my fingertips along her knuckles because it feels good to touch her skin, and I know it calms her. "Jenna, you need to understand that sometimes, the wounds are so deep they don't ever heal, not perfectly anyway. Even if you leave, even if you run away, change your whole life, new city, new people, new job, there is still going to be a Mark-sized hole in your heart. Nothing will fill it, not ever.

But you know what can ease the pain a tiny bit as time moves forward? Love. Grief is love with nowhere to go, but we can give it somewhere to go. We are still alive; we have to love everything that we have left, or we'll drown in the grief."

She tries to speak through her sobs, and it comes out all garbled, but I can still hear every word. "I am drowning, Liam! Don't you get it? I can't breathe, I can't think, I can't do this!"

I reach for her and take both of her arms in my hands and look into her eyes. "But you can, and you will. You are doing it. Look at you. Every day, you're doing it. That's what this is." I wipe her tears the best I can, but it feels so futile. Her pain is so much bigger than these tears. She's crying harder now, and it breaks my heart to see her fall apart, but I think she needs to do this to be able to be put back together.

"You will never be the same Jenna that you were before Mark died, but you are still Jenna. You told me once that you would love every version of me. Let me do the same for you. I love you, Jenna, broken or whole, happy or sad, grieving or healing. We are both all of those things all the time. Loss does that to a person, and we can't take it back."

I flip up the console so I can get closer to her, and she falls into my arms and cries, "I just don't know how Liam; I don't know how to go on."

"Let me show you then. Let me help you. Every day, we will do it together." Her head is resting on my chest, and I stroke her hair as her breathing slows to a normal pace. We sit like this for what could be minutes or hours. I don't know or care. Then she finally whispers, "Okay."

I release the breath I've been holding, "Okay?"

"I'll try. Thank you for not letting me go, Liam."

"I told you anything but that."

She lifts her head and kisses me hard on the lips. Telling me everything I need to know.

CHAPTER

Twenty-Nine

Jenna

Liam and I sit in his truck and talk for hours. I don't know why it took me so long to get to this point where I can share everything with him. There is no logic to be found in grief.

I'm sorry that I've neglected Liam's pain these last few months. I know he's lost so much, too, but I think now that he's helped me open my heart back up to him, maybe we really can work through it together.

Even when it feels impossible, he helps me to see that I can do it.

Noah and Sherri both texted to make sure we were okay. Sherri probably didn't believe Noah when he relayed Liam's reply that we were all good and just chatting. That girl has got my back like no one has before. I'm so grateful. I just showed up on her doorstep, and she welcomed me with open arms. She let me cry on her shoulder and made me feel safe and understood.

She also told me I was a complete fool and to get my ass back to Balsam River and into Liam's bed where I belong. She can always make me laugh, even when I'm in the middle of imploding my life. I don't know what I thought Liam would do when he realized I was gone, but I didn't think he would drive all the way here just to talk to me.

I don't even really feel like he drove here to talk me into coming home.

He seems to really understand what I'm going through but just won't let me go through it alone. I swear to God, this was not a test, but if it was, he passed with flying flippin' colours. This man is like none other, and I will never take that for granted again. I shift to lift my head to look into his eyes. "I'll follow you and Noah home."

His eyes widen. "Seriously? You're coming home? Today?" I can't help but laugh at him. He looks a little like a kid in a candy store.

"Yeah, I don't know what I was thinking. Well, I do, but I think I was wrong. I want to stay close and work through my emotions with you, not away from you. What do you think of leaving my house in Jamie's hands to find a tenant and bringing my suitcases to your place when we get back?"

"Jenna, I think that's all I've ever wanted. I don't want to spend a single night away from you. I want your face to be the last thing I see before I fall asleep, and I want it to be the first thing I see when I wake up. I want to make you breakfast, and I want to rub your feet on our couch. I want to cherish you and us and everything that we are, forever."

He pauses, and his eyes brighten. "You know what I really want, Jenna? More than anything?"

"There's something you want more than all that?" I smack his arm jokingly, but I'm thinking, seriously, I thought finally moving in would be everything to him.

"I want you to be my wife."

"Ha-ha, I know, I know. And I can't wait to be your wife and grow old with you, you know that! I thought you actually wanted something else." I'm laughing now because he's such a goof. It freaked me out for a second there, but I should have known; Liam's always planning for the future.

"No, my Jenny girl, I'm serious. Will you marry me?" He's pulling something out of his pocket... Oh God! Holy shit! He has a ring box in his hand.

"Jenna, I love you so much. I have loved you since I was a child, and

I will love you for as long as I live. We have learned in the hardest ways possible that we don't know how much time we have on this earth, but I can say without a doubt that I wouldn't want to spend however much time I have with anyone else but you. We can have a big wedding or a small one in the backyard; we can go to city hall or Vegas if you want. But I want this ring on your finger until that beautiful day comes. Please say you'll wear it."

Oh my God! Oh my God! This ring! He's holding a diamond ring in front of me; the diamonds are arranged in the shape of a flower. I think I'm going to throw up, but in a good way.

Oh my God, I have to answer him.

"Yes, Liam! Yes! A thousand times!" I touch the tiny flower gently with my fingertip, "It's so beautiful. So dainty and so perfect. I can't believe this, Liam." I wrap my arms around his neck and kiss him with all the love I have inside me because it all belongs to him. Tears are running down my face, and I can't stop them.

"Don't cry, babe. He's happy for us. I asked for his blessing, and then he helped me design this ring and was there with me when I picked it up."

My eyes widen in shock. "How long have you had this?"

"I was going to ask you on New Year's Day." The sadness I see in his eyes hurts my heart even more, Liam lost so much more than I thought on that day. He lost the dream he had of proposing to me, surrounded by his brothers and mine. He's been hanging on to this beautiful ring ever since. Was he afraid he would lose me, too?

"Liam, I'm so sorry I left town without talking to you. My heart breaks to think of what that must have felt like for you. I made such a horrible mistake. I can't believe this, I treat you like crap and almost jeopardize our entire relationship, and you respond by coming after me, holding me, letting me cry on your shoulder and asking me to marry you? Are you even real?"

He laughs, his deep belly laugh, and my God, it's been so long since

I've heard it; it's like music to my ears. "Why are you laughing?" I try to sound indignant, but my own laughter bubbles out of me. I can barely understand him because he's laughing so hard, but I think he says, "Will you just put the damn ring on, Jenna?"

He takes a few breaths to calm himself and looks at me with an eyebrow raised and one side of his mouth tipped up. God, I love that crooked smile as he says, "You can't help yourself, can you? You'll even argue your way out of an engagement."

"Oh no, I don't want out of it!" I snatch the ring from the box he's still holding and slide it on my finger. "I just can't believe how lucky I am. How did I find you, Liam? How did you find me?"

He leans over to kiss me again and says, "You were always meant for me. I just had to be patient."

We head back to Sherri's, and when we get there, I jump out of the truck and run to the house, but I smack right into Noah as I'm about to open the front door.

"Whoa, there, killer, slow down. Where's the fire?" He holds both of my arms so I don't fall over backwards; I shove out of his grip and throw my arms around his neck. He tentatively wraps me in a hug and says, "You okay, Jenna, what's going on?"

I was smiling, but now I'm crying again. Happy tears.

"I'm going to marry your brother."

"Well, no shit. That's not really news, but I meant, what's going on right now, that's got you so worked up?" I pull back from his hug, and my face splits into a huge grin as I hold up my left hand. "No, I mean, I'm actually going to marry your brother." I jump up and down and start squealing, and he grabs my hands and does the same.

This is Noah, always here with whatever I need. Man, I love him.

Sherri comes out the door at this exact moment and bursts out laughing. "What in God's name has got into you two?"

Liam is on the driveway, doubled over, laughing at his ridiculous brother and *fiancée*. AH!! I am a fiancée! I can't even right now. I shove my left hand into Sherri's face and scream, "Liam and I are getting married!"

Her arms are instantly around me as she says, "Yes! Jenna, you deserve this! Look at that smile. I am thanking God to see that smile on your face again. I'm so happy for you, girl."

"Thank you! Thank you for everything, you were really my soft place to land, and I couldn't have worked through all this shit inside of me without you. I appreciate you so much, and I can't wait for you to make your way back home to Balsam River; now we have a wedding to plan!"

"You bet, girlie. I need a bit more time here with my family, but I will be home before you know it." I notice her looking over at Noah. He stopped jumping and screaming around the same time that I did, but he's looking intently at Sherri now, a look I can't decipher passes between them. Maybe they had a good heart-to-heart while I was out with Liam; if it helps either of them heal from all this pain, then I'm not questioning.

"I'm gonna head home with them. Noah, will you drive my car, and I'll go with Liam?"

"Sure thing, sis. See ya back at home." He winks, steps down to the driveway, and heads to my car. He smacks Liam on the shoulder on his way by him, and I hear them murmur something to each other playfully. They both have huge grins on their faces as they say goodbye, and it makes my heart feel lighter than it's been in months.

Maybe there is room for happiness next to the sadness, like Liam said.

It still hurts, but there's room for a little bit of joy to push through past the hurt.

CHAPTER

Thirty

Jenna

We called a family dinner at the farm for the next day, and now everyone is gathered around in the large living room. I smile up at Liam as everyone is oohing and aahing over my ring. It really is so unique and so beautiful. I love it so much.

Andi is back to planning her flower girl dress and everything she will get to do when the day of the wedding comes. We haven't heard her making plans in so long. It doesn't go unnoticed by any of us. She's been doing so well; she truly amazes me every day.

Kids are just so resilient; I wouldn't believe it if I didn't see it in her every day. There are things that have knocked us on our asses, but she processes them slowly at her own pace, and then it's like she grieves it and sets it down to come back to later. In the meantime, she focuses on the beautifully simple little kid life she's living. I don't think she can grasp the profound effect this loss will have on her entire life, and I'm more than a little bit grateful that she's protected by the developmental stage her brain is at right now. She misses Mark more than any of us; in her own ways, the daily love and care he gave her, and that father-daughter bond they shared are irreplaceable. But her little heart and brain can't even fathom all the 'could've beens' that us adults are grieving. Hers is a special kind of grief that will keep hitting her in various ways, over and over again, for her entire life. So, for now, if planning a wedding with a pretty dress brings a smile to her face, then I will happily provide that wedding for her.

I apologize to Sara for bailing, and she apologizes for the way she reacted. But it goes without saying how grateful I am that she went to Liam because otherwise, he wouldn't have known where to find me. We wouldn't be celebrating together like we are now.

Everything has somehow come together in the last couple of days to be this amazing celebration of our love. "I can hardly believe that just yesterday morning, I was questioning everything," I say to no one in particular.

Sara smiles. "It's crazy, isn't it? What a rollercoaster you've been on."

"I guess that's just life, though," Noah says, "Always ups and downs, right?"

Everyone nods in unison; I think we're all reflecting on these last months and where they've taken us.

"You're right, Noah, that's life. It sounds cliche, but not for the first time; my life has changed drastically in 24 hours. This time, it was for the better, and I'm embracing that joy, but we know last time it wasn't anything like this. We were all shattered, and it felt like, beyond repair. But now we sit here together, and we can feel the joy that comes with loving each other. I don't know if I ever could have known that this was possible, without you guys to show me and guide me along this path to healing. I have so much further to travel on this journey, but I can see the road in front of me now. There are so many things that have changed..." I pause to control my voice as tears run down my face, "It breaks my fucking heart to think of living the rest of this life without my brother, but there's also so much that has stayed the same, and I want to remember those things just as much."

Liam comes up beside me and wraps his arm around my waist; he pulls me in tightly to his side and kisses the side of my head. He looks around the room at his family and then mine, joined together by two love stories that will live on forever in different ways.

He holds me tightly and says, "Mark and Amy have taught us that even in the darkness, there is still light. Light comes in so many forms: in the people we love, places we've been, the amazing things we've done, and in the memories of those we've lost. Sometimes, we have to come through the darkness to appreciate the light. In hard times, we have to look for it, chase it, grab it, and never let it go. We need to live there as much as we can. Live in the light. Don't ever forget; we're only given this one life to live.

CHECK OUT SARA AND JACK'S STORY IN FROM THE ASHES - BALSAM RIVER BOOK 2

"We never wish for tragedy, and we try to avoid it at all costs, but sometimes beauty can come from the ashes that are left behind."

Sara has been torn apart by grief and loss, she's picked herself up and carried on, only to be torn apart all over again.

This time, she can't afford to fall apart because she's been left as the legal guardian to her seven-year-old niece, Andi.

Maybe this is her chance to rise above the weight of grief that's pulling her down and find her true self amongst the ashes.

Of course, Jack is always there, always waiting to help her and to love her, if only she'll let him.

Jack Turner has been waiting for the last seven years for her to give him a chance. Now he's recruiting everyone in town to help him woo the formidable Sara Ryan.

Can he convince her there's more to life than obligations?

Can she be everything Andi needs, stay true to herself and still be there for the people she loves?

"Everyone says, grief is love, but if they'd felt this grief, they wouldn't all just walk blindly into love."

Acknowledgments

This book has been my whole life in the making, but before losing my sister last year, I didn't think it was something I would ever do. Losing her brought a new perspective to my life. A perspective that I would trade in a second to have her back, but since that's not an option, I'm going to use it to live my life the way she would've wanted and the way I wish I had lived all along.

No regrets. Take the trip, buy the cottage, eat the ice cream, and write the book.

I have some of my best friends supporting me through my grief and through this life in general. These women are my cheerleaders, and I'm so grateful to have them in my life.

Savanah, Alysen, Laura and Heather, I truly could not have done this without you, not with my sanity intact anyways.

Thank you for always being there.

Jordon and our three amazing kids have suffered through this year and a half of grief alongside me, and I know I wouldn't be where I am in my healing if it wasn't for their love and support.

Writing this story was a lot like free therapy, and I appreciate you guys walking through that with me.

To anyone who's reading this story, I want to thank you for taking the time to read my words, and in doing so joining me in this journey and I hope it brings you some peace and acceptance for your or someone else's journey with grief. It's never easy, and there's no timeline. I hope you can all let joy sit next to the sadness one day.

Blessings,

Athena

About the Author

Athena is a homeschooling mom and wife from Ontario, Canada.

She believes being the youngest of 8, in a close knit, farming family is why she values the love of family and friends above everything else.

She lives with her high school sweetheart turned husband and 3 kids on his family's horse farm and couldn't have dreamed up a better place to raise her family.

She can be found on their back deck reading or writing with coffee in hand any time of day..... as long as it's after 9am.

Growing up with her only sister as her best friend in a house with 6 brothers created an unbreakable bond, hair pulling excluded. Despite her sister's untimely death their connection lives on, even in her absence, she was the inspiration behind this book.